14 FAMOUS FAIRY TALES

14 FAMOUS FAIRY TALES
Copyright @ Forlaget Carlsen, 2003
Translation by Jean Hersholt
The Litle Mermaid is translated by H.P. Paull
Design: Christensen Grafik, Copenhagen
Cover layout: Henrik Jørgensen
Printed at Livonia Print Sia
Printed in Latvia 2018

ISBN 978-87-11-22345-1
2. edition, 9. impression/0918

www.carlsen.dk
www.lindhardtogringhof.dk

Forlaget Carlsen – et forlag under Lindhardt og Ringhof Forlag A/S, et selskab i Egmont

Hans Christian Andersen

14 famous
FAIRY TALES

Illustrations by Mads Stage

CARLSEN

Contents

The Little Mermaid

Far away, where the ocean is as blue as the prettiest cornflower, and as clear as crystal, it is very, very deep; deeper than the length of any rope: many church steeples, piled one upon another, would not reach from the seabed beneath to the surface above the water. Here resides the Sea King and his subjects.

It is wrong to imagine that nothing exists at the bottom of the sea but bare yellow sand. No, indeed; the most remarkable flowers and plants grow there; the leaves and stems of which are so supple, that the slightest movement of the water causes them to stir as if they had life. Fishes, both large and small, glide between the branches, as birds fly among the trees here upon land. In the very depth of it all, stands the castle of the Sea King. Its walls are built of coral, and the long, gothic windows are of the clearest amber. The shells forming the roof, open and close as the water flows over them. They appear very beautiful, for in each lies a splendid pearl, fit for the diadem of a queen.

The Sea King had been a widower for many years, and his aged mother kept house for him. She was a very wise woman, and exceedingly proud of her high birth; on that account she wore twelve oysters on her tail; while others, also of high rank, were only allowed to wear six. She did, however, deserve great praise, especially for her care of the little sea-princesses, her grand-daughters. They were six beautiful children; and the youngest was the prettiest of them all; her skin was as clear and delicate as a rose-petal, and her eyes as blue as the deepest sea; but, like all the others, she had no feet, and her body ended in a fish's tail.

All day long they played in the great halls of the castle, or among the living flowers that grew out of the walls. The large amber windows were open, and the fish swam in, just as the swallows fly into our houses when we open the windows, only the fishes would swim up to the princesses, eat out of their hands, and allowed themselves to be stroked.

Outside the castle there was a beautiful garden, in which grew bright red and dark blue flowers, and blossoms like flames of fire; the fruit glittered like gold, and the leaves and stems waved to and fro continually. The ground itself was the finest sand, only blue as the flame of burning sulphur. An extraordinary blue lustre surrounded the place, as if it really were situated in the sky above, instead of the dark depths of the sea. In calm weather the sun could be seen, looking like a purple flower, with the light flowing from the calyx.

Each of the young princesses had a little plot of ground in the garden, where she might dig and plant as she pleased. One arranged her flower-bed into the form of a whale; another thought it better to make hers like the figure of a little mermaid; but that of the youngest was round like the sun, and consisted of flowers as red as his rays at sunset. She was a strange child, quiet and thoughtful; and while her sisters would be delighted with the wonderful things which they obtained from the wrecks of vessels, she only cared for her pretty red flowers, resembling the sun, and a beautiful marble statue. It was the representation of a handsome boy, carved out of pure white stone, which had fallen to the bottom of the sea from a wreck. She planted by the statue a rose-coloured weeping willow. It grew splendidly, and very soon drooped its fresh branches over the statue, almost down to the blue sands. The shadow had a violet tint, and like the branches, it waved to and fro; as if the crown of the tree and the root were at play, and trying to kiss each other.

Nothing gave her so much pleasure as to hear about the world above the sea. She made her old grandmother tell her all she knew of the ships and of the towns, the people and the animals. Most of all it seemed to her enchantingly beautiful to hear that the flowers of the land should have fragrance, unlike those below the sea; that the trees of the forest should be green; and that the fishes among the trees could sing so sweetly, that it was quite a pleasure to hear them. The grandmother called the little birds fishes, or she would not have understood her; for she had never seen birds.

»When you have reached your fifteenth year,« said the grandmother, »you will have permission to rise up out of the sea, to sit on the rocks in the moon-light, while the great ships are sailing by; and then you will see both forests and towns.« In the following year, one of the sisters would be fifteen. As each sister was a year younger than the other, the youngest would have to wait five years before her turn came to rise up from the bottom of the ocean, and see the earth as we do. However, each promised to tell the others what she saw on her first visit, and what she thought the most beautiful; for their grandmother could not tell them enough; there were so many things they wanted to know.

The youngest longed more than the rest for her turn to come, she who had

the longest time to wait, and who was so quiet and thoughtful. Many nights she stood by the open window, looking up through the dark blue water, and watching the fish as they splashed about with their fins and tails. She could see the moon and stars shining faintly; and through the water they looked larger than they do to our eyes. Then something like a black cloud passed between her and them, she knew that it was either a whale swimming over her head, or a ship full of human beings, who never imagined that a pretty little mermaid was standing beneath them, reaching out her white hands towards the keel of their ship.

As soon as the eldest was fifteen, she was allowed to rise to the surface of the ocean. When she came back, she had hundreds of things to talk about; but the most beautiful, she said, was to lie in the moonlight, on a sandbank, in the quiet sea, near the coast, and to gaze upon a large town nearby, where the lights were twinkling like hundreds of stars; to listen to the sounds of the music, the noise of carriages, and the voices of human beings, and then to hear the merry bells ringing out from the church steeples; and because she could not go near to all those wonderful things, she longed for them more than ever.

Oh, how the youngest sister listened eagerly to all the accounts, and afterwards, when she stood at the open window looking up through the dark blue water, she thought of the great city, with all its bustle and noise, and even fancied she could hear the sound of the church bells, down in the depths of the sea.

In another year the second sister received permission to rise to the surface of the water, and to swim about where she pleased. She rose just as the sun was setting, and this, she said, was the most beautiful sight of all. The whole sky looked like gold, while violet and rose-coloured clouds, which she could not describe, floated over her; and, still more rapidly than the clouds, flew a large flock of wild swans towards the setting sun, looking like a long white veil across the sea. She also swam towards the sun; but it sunk into the waves, and the rosy tints faded from the clouds and the sea.

The third sister's turn followed; she was the boldest of them all, and she swam up a broad river that emptied itself into the sea. On the banks she saw green hills covered with beautiful vines; palaces and castles peeped out between the proud trees of the forest; she heard the birds singing, and the rays of the sun were so powerful that she was often obliged to dive down under the water to cool her burning face. In a narrow creek she found a group of little human children, quite naked fooling about in the water; she wanted to play with them, but they fled in fear; then a little black animal appeared; it was a dog, but she did not know that, for she had never before seen one. This animal barked at her so terribly that she became frightened, and rushed back to the open sea. But she said she should never forget the beautiful forest, the green hills, and the lovely little children who could swim in the water, although they did not have fish tails.

The fourth sister was more timid; she remained in the midst of the sea, but she said it was just as beautiful there as nearer the land. She could see for so many miles around her, and the sky above looked like a dome of glass. She had seen the ships, but at such a great distance that they looked like sea-gulls. The dolphins frolicked in the waves, and the great whales spouted water from their blow holes till it seemed as if she were surrounded by a hundred fountains.

The fifth sister's birthday was in the winter; so when her turn came, she saw what the others had not seen the first time they went up. The sea looked quite green, and large icebergs were floating about, each like a pearl, she said, but far greater than the churches built by men. They were of the most wondrous shapes, glittering like diamonds. She had seated herself upon one of the largest, and let the wind play with her long hair, and she noticed that all the ships sailed by rapidly, and steered as far away as they could from the iceberg, as if they were afraid of it. Towards evening, as the sun went down, dark clouds covered the sky, the thunder rolled and the lightning flashed, and the red light glowed on the icebergs as they rocked and tossed on the heaving sea. On all the ships the sails were reefed in alarm and fear, while she sat calmly on the floating iceberg, watching the blue lightning, as it darted its forked flashes into the sea.

Once the sisters had been permitted to rise to the surface, they were each delighted with the new and beautiful sights they saw. And now, being grown-up girls, and able to go when they pleased, they only seemed to lose interest. They wished themselves back again in the water, and after a month had passed they said it was much more beautiful down below, and nice to be at home.

Yet often, in the evening hours, the five sisters would join hands, and rise to the surface. Their voices were more beautiful than any human being's; and before the approach of a storm, when they expected a ship would be lost, they swam before the vessel, and sang sweetly of the delights to be found in the depths of the sea, begging the sailors not to fear if they sank to the bottom. But the sailors could not understand the song, they mistook it for the howling of the storm. These things were never to be beautiful to them; for if the ship sank, the men were drowned, and only their dead bodies reached the palace of the Sea King.

When the sisters would rise, arm-in-arm, through the water, their youngest sister stood all alone, watching them, about to cry, only mermaids have no tears, and therefore suffer more.

»Oh, were I but fifteen years old,« said she, »I know that I shall love the world up there, and all the people who live in it.«

At last she reached her fifteenth year.

»Well, now, you are grown up,« said the old dowager, her grand-mother; »so you must let me adorn you like your other sisters;« and she placed a wreath of white lilies in her hair, and every petal was half a pearl. Then the old lady ordered eight great oysters to attach themselves to the princess' tail demonstrating her high rank.

»But they hurt me so,« said the little mermaid.

»Pride must suffer pain,« replied the old lady.

Oh, how gladly she would have shaken off all this grandeur, and laid aside the heavy wreath! The red flowers in her own garden would have suited her much better, but she did not have the courage to oppose. So she said, »farewell,« and rose as lightly as a bubble to the surface of the water.

The sun had just set as she raised her head above the waves; the clouds were tinted with crimson and gold, and through the glimmering twilight beamed the evening star in all its beauty. The sea was calm, and the air mild and fresh. A large ship, with three masts, lay still on the water, with only one sail set; not a breeze stirred, and the sailors sat idle on deck or amongst the rigging. There was music and song on board; and, as darkness fell, a hundred coloured lanterns were lit, as if the flags of all nations waved in the air. The little mermaid swam close to the cabin windows; and now and then, as the waves lifted her up, she could peak through clear glass window-panes, and see a number of well-dressed people within. Among them was a young prince, the most beautiful of all, with large black eyes; he was sixteen years of age, his birthday was being celebrated with much excitement. The sailors were dancing on deck, and when the prince came out of the cabin, more than a hundred rockets rose into the air, turning it as bright as day. The little mermaid was so startled that she dived under water; and when she again reared her head, it appeared as if all the stars of heaven were falling around her, she had never seen such fireworks before. Great suns spurted fire about, splendid fireflies flew into the blue air, and everything was reflected in the clear, calm sea beneath. The ship itself was so brightly illuminated that all the people, and even the smallest rope, could be seen distinctly. And how handsome the young prince looked, as he shook the hands of all present and smiled at them, while the music sounded in the clear night air.

It was very late; yet the little mermaid could not take her eyes off the ship, or the beautiful prince. The coloured lanterns had been extinguished, no more rockets rose in the air, and the cannon had ceased firing. The sea became restless, and a moaning, grumbling sound could be heard beneath the waves: still the little mermaid remained by the cabin window, bobbing up and down on the water, enabling her to look in. After a while, the sails were quickly unfurled, and the noble ship continued her journey; but soon the waves rose higher, heavy clouds darkened the sky, and lightning appeared in the distance. A dreadful storm was approaching; once more the sails were

reefed, and the great ship pursued her flying course over the raging sea. The waves grew as high as mountains, as if they wanted to overtop the mast; but the ship dived like a swan between them, and then rose again on their towering, foaming crests. To the little mermaid this appeared pleasant sport; not so to the sailors. At length the ship groaned and creaked; the thick planks gave way under the lashing of the sea as it crashed down upon the deck; the mainmast snapped in two like a reed; the ship lay over on her side; and water poured in. The little mermaid now understood that the crew were in danger; even she had to be careful to avoid the beams and planks of the wreck that lay scattered in the water. One moment all was so pitch black that she could not

see a single object, then a flash of lightning revealed the whole scene; she could see every member of the ship except the prince. When the ship parted, she had seen him sink into the deep waves, and she was glad, for she thought he would now be with her; and then she remembered that human beings could not live in the water, and when he reached her father's palace he would be quite dead. But he must not die. So she swam about among the beams and planks scattered on the surface of the sea, forgetting that they could crush her to pieces. Then she dived deeply under the dark waters, rising and falling with the waves, till at length she managed to find the young prince, who was fast losing the ability to swim in that stormy sea. His limbs were failing him, his beautiful eyes were closed, and he would have died had the little mermaid not

come to his assistance. She held his head above the water, and let the waves carry them where they pleased.

In the morning the storm had ceased; but not a single fragment of the ship could be seen. The sun rose up red and glowing from the water, and its beams brought back a healthy colour to the prince's cheeks; but his eyes remained closed. The mermaid kissed his high, smooth forehead, and stroked back his wet hair; he seemed to her like the marble statue in her little garden, and she kissed him again, wishing that he might live.

Presently they came in sight of land; she saw tall blue mountains, on which the white snow rested as if a flock of swans were lying upon them. Near the coast were beautiful green forests, and close by stood a large building, she could not tell if it was a church or a convent. Orange and lemon trees grew in the garden, and before the door stood noble palms. The sea here formed a little bay, in which the water was quite still, but very deep; so she swam with the handsome prince to the beach, which was covered with fine, white sand, and there she laid him in the warm sunshine, taking care to raise his head higher than his body.

Then bells sounded in the large white building, and a number of young girls came into the garden. The little mermaid swam from the shore and placed herself between some high rocks that rose out of the water; then she covered her head and neck with the foam of the sea so that her little face might not be seen, as she watched to see what would become of the poor prince.

She did not wait long before she saw a young girl approach the spot where he lay. She seemed frightened at first, but only for a moment; then she fetched a number of people, and the mermaid saw that the prince came to life again, and smiled at those who stood round him. But to her he sent no smile; he did not know that she had saved him. This made her very unhappy, and when he was led away into the great building, she dived sorrowfully down into the water, and returned to her father's palace.

She had always been silent and thoughtful, now more so than ever. Her sisters asked her what she had seen during her first visit to the surface of the water; but she would tell them nothing.

Many an evening and morning did she rise to the place where she had left the prince. She saw the fruits in the garden ripen till they were gathered, the snow on the tops of the mountains melt away; but she never saw the prince, and therefore she returned home, each time more sorrowful than before. Her only comfort was to sit in her own little garden, and fling her arm round the beautiful marble statue which was like the prince. She gave up tending her flowers, and they grew in wild confusion over the paths, twining their long leaves and stems round the branches of the trees, so that the whole place became dark and gloomy.

Finally she could not bear it any longer, and told one of her sisters all about it. Then the others heard the secret, and very soon it became known to two mermaids whose close friend happened to know who the prince was. She had also seen the celebration on board ship, and she told them where the prince came from, and where to find his palace.

»Come, little sister,« said the other princesses; then they joined hands and rose up in a long row to the surface of the water, close to the spot where they knew the prince's palace stood.

It was built of bright yellow shining stone, with long flights of marble steps, one of which reached nearly down to the sea. Splendid gilded domes rose over the roof, and between the pillars that surrounded the whole building stood life-like statues of marble. Through the clear crystal of the tall windows could be seen noble rooms, with costly silk curtains and hangings of tapestry; and the walls were covered with beautiful paintings, which were pleasing to look at. In the centre of the largest saloon a fountain spurting its sparkling jets high up into the glass dome of the ceiling. The sun shone down through the dome upon the water and the beautiful plants growing round the basin of the fountain.

Now that she knew where he lived, she spent many an evening and many a night in the sea near the palace. She would swim much nearer the shore than any of the others ventured to do; indeed once she went quite up the narrow channel under the marble balcony, which threw an immense shadow on the water. Here she would sit, watching the young prince, who thought himself all alone in the bright moonlight.

She saw him many times of an evening sailing in a pleasant boat, with music playing and flags waving. She peeped out from among the green rushes, and if the wind caught her long silvery-white veil, those who saw it believed it to be a swan, spreading out its wings.

On many a night, too, when the fishermen, with their torches, were out at sea, she heard them relate so many good things about the doings of the young prince, that she was glad she had saved his life when he had been tossed about half-dead on the waves. And she remembered that his head had rested on her bosom, and how warmly she had kissed him; but he knew nothing of this, and could not even dream of her.

She grew more and more fond of human beings, and wished more and more to be able to wander about with them in their world which seemed to be so much larger than her own. They could fly over the sea in ships, and mount the high hills which were far above the clouds; and the lands they possessed, their woods and their fields, stretched far away beyond the reach of her sight. There was so much that she wanted to know, and her sisters were unable to answer all her questions. Then she implored her old grandmother, who knew all about the upper world, which she very rightly called the lands above the sea.

»If human beings are not drowned,« asked the little mermaid, »can they live forever? do they never die as we do here in the sea?«

»Yes,« replied the old lady, »they must also die, and their term of life is even shorter than ours. We sometimes live to three hundred years, but when we cease to exist here we merely become foam on the surface of the water, down here we have not even a grave of those we love. We do not have immortal souls, we shall never live again; but, like the green seaweed, when once it has been cut off, we can never flourish again. Human beings, on the contrary, have a soul, which lives forever, lives after the body has turned to dust. It rises up through the clear, pure air beyond the glittering stars. As we rise out of the water, and behold all the land of the earth, they do rise to unknown and glorious regions which we shall never see.«

»Why do we not have an immortal soul?« asked the little mermaid mournfully; »I would give gladly all the hundreds of years that I have to live, to be a human being only for one day. To have the hope of knowing the happiness of that glorious world above the stars.«

»You must not think of that,« said the old lady; »we feel ourselves to be much happier and much better off than human beings.«

»So I shall die,« said the little mermaid, »and as the foam of the sea I shall be driven about never again to hear the music of the waves, or to see the pretty flowers nor the red sun. Is there anything I can do to win an immortal soul?«

»No,« said the old lady, »unless a man were to love you so much that you were more to him than his father or mother. If all his thoughts and all his love were fixed upon you and the priest placed his right hand in yours, and he promised to be true to you here and hereafter. Then his soul would glide into your body and you would obtain a share in the future happiness of mankind. He would give a soul to you and retain his own as well; but this can never happen. Your fish tail, which amongst us is considered so beautiful, is thought on earth to be quite ugly; they do not know any better, and they think it necessary to have two stout supports, which they call legs, in order to be handsome.«

Then the little mermaid sighed, and looked dismally at her fish tail.

»Let us be happy,« said the old lady, »and dart and spring about during the three hundred years that we have to live, which is really quite long enough; after that we can go to rest, contended. This evening we are going to have a royal ball.«

It is one of those splendid sights, which we can never see on earth. The walls and the ceiling of the large ballroom were of thick, but transparent crystal. May hundreds of colossal shells, some of a deep red, others of a grass green, stood on each side in rows, with blue fire in them, which lighted up the whole saloon, and shone through the walls, so that the sea was also illuminated. Innumerable fishes, great and small, swam past the crystal walls; on some of them the scales glowed with a purple brilliancy, and on others they shone like silver and gold. Through the halls flowed a broad stream, and in it danced the mermen and the mermaids to the music of their own sweet singing. No one on earth has such lovely voices as they. The little mermaid sang more sweetly than the rest. The whole court applauded her with hands and tails; and for a moment her heart felt quite joyful, for she knew she had the loveliest voice of any on earth or in the sea. But she soon thought again of the world above her, for she could not forget the charming prince, nor her sorrow that she had not an immortal soul like his. Therefore she crept away silently out of her father's palace, and while everything within was gladness and song, she sat in her own little garden sorrowful and alone. Then she heard the bugle sounding through the water, and thought, »it is certainly him sailing above, he holds my every wish, in his hands I should like to place the happiness of my life. I will venture all for him, and to win an immortal soul, while my sisters dance in my father's palace, I will go to the sea witch, of whom I have always been so much afraid, but she can give me counsel and help.«

And then the little mermaid went out from her garden, and took the road to the foaming whirlpools, behind which the sorceress lived. She had never been that way before: neither flowers nor grass grew there; nothing but bare, grey, sandy ground stretched out to the whirlpool, where the water, like foaming mill-wheels, whirled round everything that it seized, and cast it into the fathomless deep. Through the midst of these crushing whirlpools the little mermaid was obliged to pass, to reach the dominions of the sea witch; and also for a long distance the only road lay right across a quantity of warm, bubbling mire, the witch called her marshes. Beyond this stood her house, in the centre of a strange forest, in which all the trees and flowers were polypi, half animals and half plants; they looked like serpents with a hundred heads growing out of the ground. The branches were long slimy arms, with fingers like flexible worms, moving limb after limb from the root to the top. All that could be reached in the sea they seized upon, and held fast, so that it never escaped from their clutches. The little mermaid was so alarmed at what she saw, that she stood still, and her heart beat with fear, and she very nearly turned back; but she thought of the prince, and of the human soul she longed for, and her courage returned. She fastened her long flowing hair round her head, so that the polypi couldn't seize hold of it. She folded her arms across her bosom, and then she darted forward as a fish shoots through the water, between the supple arms and fingers of the ugly polypi, which were stretched out on each side of her. She saw that each held in its grasp something it had seized with its numerous little arms, as if they were iron bands. The white skeletons of human beings perished at sea, and had sunk down into the deep waters, skeletons of land animals, oars, rudders, and chests of ships were lying tightly grasped by their clinging arms; even a little mermaid, whom they had caught and strangled. This seemed the most shocking of all to the little princess.

She now came to a space of boggy ground in the wood, where large, fat water-snakes were rolling in the mire, and showing their ugly, drab-coloured bodies. In the midst of this spot stood a house, built with the bones of shipwrecked human beings. There sat the sea witch, allowing a toad to eat from her mouth, just as people sometimes feed a canary with a piece of sugar. She called the ugly water-snakes her little chickens, and allowed them to crawl all over her bosom.

»I know what you want,« said the sea witch; »it is very stupid of you, but you shall have your way, and it will bring you to sorrow, my pretty princess. You want to get rid of your fish tail, and to have two supports instead of it, like human beings on earth, so that the young prince may fall in love with you, and that you may have an immortal soul.« And then the witch laughed so loudly and horribly, that the toad and the snakes fell to the ground, and lay there wriggling about. »You are just in time,« said the witch, »for after sunrise tomorrow I should not be able to help you until the end of another year. I will prepare a draught for you, with which you must swim to land tomorrow before sunrise, and sit down on the shore and drink it. Your tail will then disappear, and shrink up into what mankind calls legs, and you will feel great pain, as if a sword were passing through you. But all that see you, will say that you are the prettiest little human being they ever saw. You will still have the same floating gracefulness of movement, and no dancer will ever tread so lightly; but at every step you take it will feel as if you were treading upon sharp knives, and blood must flow. If you will bear all this, I will help you.«

»Yes, I will,« said the little princess in a trembling voice, as she thought of the prince and the immortal soul.

»But think again,« said the witch, »for when once your shape has become like a human being, you can no more be a mermaid. You will never return through the water to your sisters, or to your father's palace again. If you do not win the love of the prince, so that he is willing to forget his father and mother for your sake, and to love you with his whole soul, and allow the priest to join your hands that you may be man and wife, then you will never have an immortal soul. The first morning after he marries another your heart will break, and you will become foam on the crest of the waves.«

»I will do it,« said the little mermaid, turning pale as death.

»But I must be paid also,« said the witch, »and it is not a trifle that I ask. You have the sweetest voice of any that dwell here in the depths of the sea. You believe that you will be able to charm the prince with it also, but this voice you must give to me; the best thing you possess will I have for the price of my

draught. My own blood must be mixed with it, that it may be as sharp as a two-edged sword.«

»But if you take away my voice,« said the little mermaid, »what is left for me?«

»Your beautiful form, your graceful walk, and your expressive eyes; surely with these you can enchain a man's heart. Well, have you lost your courage? Poke out your little tongue that I may cut it off as my payment; then you shall have the powerful draught.«

»It shall be done,« said the little mermaid. Then the witch placed her cauldron on the fire, to prepare the magic draught. »Cleanliness is a good thing,« said she, scouring the vessel with snakes, which she had tied together in a large knot; then she pricked herself in the breast, and let the black blood drop into it. The steam that rose formed such horrible shapes that no one could look at them without fear. Every moment the witch threw something else into the cauldron, and when it began to boil, it sounded like the weeping of a crocodile. When at last the magic draught was ready, it looked like the clearest water.

»This is for you,« said the witch. Then she cut off the mermaid's tongue, so that she became dumb, and would never speak or sing again.

»If the polypi should seize hold of you as you return through the wood,« said the witch, »throw over them a few drops of the potion, and their fingers will be torn into a thousand pieces.« But the little mermaid had no need to do this, for the polypi sprang back in terror when they caught sight of the glittering draught, which shone in her hand like a twinkling star. So she passed quickly through the wood and the marsh, and between the rushing whirlpools.

She saw that in her father's palace the torches in the ballroom were extinguished and all within asleep; but she did not venture to go in to them, for now she was dumb and going to leave them forever, she felt as if her heart would break. She crept into the garden, took a flower from the flowerbeds of each of her sisters, kissed her hand a thousand times towards the palace, and then rose up through the dark blue waters.

The sun had not yet risen when she came in sight of the prince's palace, and approached the beautiful marble steps, but the moon shone clear and bright. Then the little mermaid drank the magic draught, and it seemed as if a two-edged sword went through her delicate body: she fainted, and lay as still as the dead. When the sun arose and shone over the sea, she recovered, and felt a sharp pain; but just before her stood the handsome young prince. He fixed his jet-black eyes upon her so earnestly that she cast down her own. Then she became aware that her fish tail was gone, and that she had as pretty a pair of white legs and tiny feet as any little maiden could have; but she had no clothes, so she wrapped herself in her long, thick hair. The prince asked her who she was, and where she came from. She looked at him with gentle and sad deep blue eyes; but she could not speak. Every step she took was as the witch said it would be. She felt as if she were treading upon the points of needles or sharp knives; but she bore it willingly, and stepped as lightly by the prince's side as a bubble, so that he and all that saw her wondered at her graceful-swaying movements.

She was very soon dressed in costly robes of silk and muslin, and was the most beautiful creature in the palace; but she was dumb, and could neither speak nor sing.

Beautiful female slaves, dressed in silk and gold, stepped forward and sang before the prince and his royal parents: one sang better than all the others, and the prince clapped his hands and smiled at her. This saddened the little mermaid; she knew how much more sweetly she once could sing, and she thought, »oh if only he knew! I have given away my voice forever, to be with him.«

The slaves next performed some pretty fairy-like dances, to the sound of beautiful music. Then the little mermaid raised her lovely white arms, stood on the tips of her toes, and glided over the floor, and danced as no one yet had been able to dance. Each moment her beauty became more revealed, and her expressive eyes appealed more directly to the heart than the songs of the slaves.

Every one was enchanted, especially the prince, who called her his little waif; she danced again quite readily, to please him, though each time her foot touched the floor it seemed as if she was stepping on sharp knives. The prince said she should remain with him always, and she received permission to sleep at his door, on a velvet cushion.

He had a page's dress made for her, that she might accompany him on horseback. They rode together through the sweet-scented woods, where the green boughs touched their shoulders, and the little birds sang among the fresh leaves. She climbed with the prince to the tops of high mountains; and although her tender feet bled so that even her steps were marked, she only laughed, and followed him till they could see the clouds beneath them like a flock of birds travelling to distant lands.

At the prince's palace, and when all the household were asleep, she would go and sit on the broad marble steps; for it eased her burning feet to bathe them in the cold sea-water; and then she thought of all those down below in the ocean.

Once during the night her sisters came up arm-in-arm, singing sadly, as they floated on the water. She beckoned to them. They recognized her, and told her how she had grieved them. After that, they came to the same place every night; and once she saw in the distance her old grandmother, who had not been to the surface of the sea for many years, and the old Sea King, her father, with his crown on his head. They stretched out their hands towards her, but they did not venture so near the land as her sisters did.

As the days passed, she loved the prince more fondly, and he loved her as he would love a little child. But it never entered his head to make her his wife; yet, unless he married her, she could not receive an immortal soul; and, on the morning after his marriage to another, she would dissolve into the foam of the sea.

»Do you not love me the best of them all?« the eyes of the little mermaid seemed to say, when he took her in his arms, and kissed her fair forehead.

»Yes, you are dear to me,« said the prince, »for you have the best heart, and you are the most devoted to me; you are like a young maiden whom I once saw, but whom I shall never meet again. I was in a ship that was wrecked, and the waves cast me ashore near a holy temple, where several young maidens performed the service. The youngest of them found me on the shore, and saved my life. I saw her but twice, and she is the only one in the world whom I could love; but you are like her, and you have almost driven her image out of my mind. She belongs to the holy temple, and my good fortune has sent you to me instead of her; and we will never part.«

»Ah, he does not know that it was I who saved his life,« thought the little mermaid. »I carried him over the sea to the wood where the temple stands: I sat beneath the foam, and watched till the human beings came to help him. I saw the pretty maiden that he loves more than he loves me;« and the

mermaid sighed deeply, but she could not shed tears. »He says the maiden belongs to the holy temple, therefore she will never return to the world. They will not meet again. I am by his side, and see him every day. I will take care of him, and love him, and give up my life for his sake.«

Very soon a fine ship was being fitted out as it was said that the prince must marry, and that the beautiful daughter of a neighbouring king would be his wife. Although the prince gave out that he merely intended to pay a visit to the king, it was generally supposed that he really went to see his daughter. An immense company were to go with him. The little mermaid smiled, and shook her head. She knew the prince's thoughts better than anyone else did. »I must travel,« he had said to her, »I must see this beautiful princess; my parents desire it; but they will not make me bring her home as my bride. I cannot love her; she is not like the beautiful maiden in the temple, whom you resemble. If I were forced to choose a bride, I would rather choose you, my dumb waif, with those expressive eyes.« And then he kissed her rosy mouth, played with her long waving hair, and laid his head close to her heart, while she dreamed of human happiness and an immortal soul.

»You are not afraid of the sea, my dumb child,« said he, as they stood on the deck of the noble ship, which was to carry them to the country of the neighbouring king. And then he told her of storm and of calm, of strange fishes in the deep beneath them, and of what the divers had seen there. She smiled at his descriptions, for she knew better than any one what wonders were to be found at the bottom of the sea.

In the moonlight, when all on board were asleep, except the man at the helm, who was steering, she sat on the deck, gazing down through the clear water. She thought she could distinguish her father's palace, and upon it her aged grandmother, with the silver crown on her head, looking through the surge of water at the keel of the vessel. Then her sisters came up on the waves, and gazed at her mournfully, wringing their white hands. She beckoned to them, and smiled, wanting to tell them how happy and well off she was; but the cabin boy approached, and when her sisters dived down he thought all he was seeing was the foam of the sea.

The next morning the ship sailed into the harbour of a beautiful town belonging to the king whom the prince was going to visit. The church bells were ringing, and from the high towers sounded a flourish of trumpets; and soldiers, with flying colours and glittering bayonets, lined the rocks through which they passed. Every day was a celebration; balls and entertainment followed one another. But the princess had not yet appeared. People said that she was being brought up and educated in a religious house, where she was learning every royal virtue. At last she came.

Then the little mermaid, who was very anxious to see whether she was really beautiful, was obliged to acknowledge that she had never seen a more perfect vision of beauty. Her skin was delicately fair, and beneath her long dark eyelashes her laughing blue eyes shone with truth and purity.

»It was you,« said the prince, »who saved my life when I lay dead on the beach,« and he held his blushing bride in his arms. »Oh, I am too happy,« said he to the little mermaid; »my highest hopes are all fulfilled. You will rejoice at my happiness; for your devotion to me is great and sincere.« The little mermaid kissed his hand, and felt as if her heart was already broken. His wedding morning would bring death to her, and she would turn into the foam of the sea.

Every church bell rang out and the heralds rode about the town proclaiming the engagement. Perfumed oil was burning in costly silver lamps on every altar. The priests waved the censers, while the bride and bridegroom joined their hands and received the blessing of the bishop. The little mermaid, dressed in silk and gold, held up the bride's train. But her ears heard nothing of the festive music, and her eyes did not see the holy ceremony; she thought of the night of death ahead of her, and of all she had lost in the world.

On the same evening the bride and bridegroom went on board ship. Cannons were roaring, flags waving, and in the centre of the ship a costly tent of purple and gold had been erected. It contained elegant couches, for the reception of the bridal pair during the night.

The ship, with swelling sails and a favourable wind, glided away smoothly and lightly over the calm sea.

When it grew dark a number of coloured lamps were lit, and the sailors danced merrily on the deck. The little mermaid could not help thinking of her first rising out of the sea, when she had seen similar festivities and joys; and she joined in the dance, poised herself in the air like a swallow when he pursues his prey, and all present cheered her with wonder. She had never danced so elegantly before. Her tender feet felt as if cut with sharp knives, but she did not mind; a sharper pang had pierced through her heart. She knew this was the last evening she should ever see the prince, for whom she had abandoned her kindred and her home; she had given up her beautiful voice, and suffered unheard-of pain daily for him, while he knew nothing of it. This was the last evening that she would breathe the same air with him, or gaze at the starry sky and the deep sea; an eternal night, without thought or dream, awaited her: she had no soul and now she could never gain one. All was joy and gayety on board ship till long after midnight, she laughed and danced with the rest, while thoughts of death were in her heart. The prince kissed his beautiful bride, as she played with his raven hair, till they went hand in hand to rest in the splendid tent.

Then all became still on board the ship, only the helmsman stood awake at the helm. The little mermaid leaned her white arms on the edge of the vessel, and looked towards the east for the first blush of morning, for that first ray of dawn that would bring her death. She saw her sisters rising out of the flood: they were as pale as herself; but their long beautiful hair waved no more in the wind, and had been cut off.

»We have given our hair to the witch,« said they, »to help you, so that you may not die tonight. She has given us a knife: here it is, see it is very sharp. Before the sun rises you must plunge it into the prince's heart. When the warm blood falls upon your feet they will grow together again, forming into a fish tail, and you will once more become a mermaid, and return to us to live for three hundred years before you die and change into the salty foam of the sea. Hurry, now; he or you must die before sunrise. Our old grandmother moans so for you, that her white hair is falling off from sorrow, as ours fell under the witch's scissors. Kill the prince and come back; hurry: don't you see the first red streaks in the sky? In a few minutes the sun will rise, and you will die.« And then they sighed deeply and mournfully, and sank down beneath the waves.

The little mermaid drew back the crimson curtain of the tent, and beheld the fair bride with her head resting on the prince's breast. She bent down and kissed his fair brow, then looked at the sky on which the rosy dawn grew brighter and brighter; then she glanced at the sharp knife, and again fixed her eyes on the prince, who whispered the name of his bride in his dreams. She was in his thoughts, the knife trembled in the hand of the little mermaid: then she flung it far away from her into the waves; the water turned red where it fell, and the drops that spurted up looked like blood. She cast one more long, weakening glance at the prince, and then threw herself from the ship into the sea, and felt her body was dissolving into foam.

The sun rose above the waves, and his warm rays fell on the cold foam of the little mermaid. She did not feel as if she were dying. She saw the bright sun, and all around her floated hundreds of transparent beautiful beings. Through them she could see the white sails of the ship, and the red clouds in the sky; their speech was melodious, but too ethereal to be heard by mortal ears, as they were also unseen by mortal eyes. The little mermaid perceived that she had a body like theirs, and that she continued to rise higher and higher out of the foam.

»Where am I?« asked she, and her voice sounded ethereal, as the voice of those who were with her; no earthly music could imitate it.

»Among the daughters of the air,« answered one of them. »A mermaid does not have an immortal soul, nor can she obtain one unless she wins the love of a human being. Her eternal destiny depends on the power of another. The daughters of the air do not possess an immortal soul, but can however, by their good deeds, procure one for themselves. We fly to warm countries, and cool the sultry air that destroys mankind with the pestilence. We carry the perfume of the flowers to spread health and restoration. After we have endeavoured for three hundred years at the best of our abilities, we receive an immortal soul and take part in the happiness of mankind. You, poor little mermaid, have tried with your whole heart to do as we are doing; you have suffered and endured and raised yourself to the spirit-world by your good deeds; and now, by striving for three hundred years in the same way, you may obtain an immortal soul.«

The little mermaid lifted her glorified eyes towards the sun, and felt them, for the first time, filling with tears. On the ship, in which she had left the prince, there was activity and noise; she saw him and his beautiful bride searching for her; mournfully they gazed at the pearly foam, as if they knew she had thrown herself into the waves. Unseen she kissed the forehead of the bride, and fanned the prince, and then rose with the other children of the air to a rosy cloud that floated through the ether.

»So for three hundred years we shall float like this,« said the little mermaid, »till at last we come into the kingdom of heaven.«

»And we may even get there sooner,« whispered one of her companions. »Unseen we can enter the houses of men, where there are children, and for every day we find a good child, who is the joy of his parents and deserves their love, our time of probation is shortened. The child does not know, when we fly through the room, that we smile with joy at his good behaviour, for we can count one year less of our three hundred years. But when we see a naughty or a wicked child, we shed tears of sorrow, and for every tear a day is added to our time of trial!«

The Princess on the Pea

Once there was a Prince who wanted to marry a Princess. Only a real one would do. So he traveled through all the world to find her, and everywhere things went wrong. There were Princesses aplenty, but how was he to know whether they were real Princesses? There was something not quite right about them all. So he came home again and was unhappy, because he did so want to have a real Princess.

One evening a terrible storm blew up. It lightened and thundered and rained. It was really frightful! In the midst of it all came a knocking at the town gate. The old King went to open it.

Who should be standing outside but a Princess, and what a sight she was in all that rain and wind. Water streamed from her hair down her clothes into her shoes, and ran out at the heels. Yet she claimed to be a real Princess.

»We'll soon find that out,« the old Queen thought to herself. Without saying a word about it she went to the bedchamber, stripped back the bedclothes, and put just one pea in the bottom of the bed. Then she took twenty mattresses and piled them on the pea. Then she took twenty eiderdown feather beds and piled them on the mattresses. Up on top of all these the Princess was to spend the night.

In the morning they asked her, »Did you sleep well?«

»Oh!« said the Princess. »No. I scarcely slept at all. Heaven knows what's in that bed. I lay on something so hard that I'm black and blue all over. It was simply terrible.«

They could see she was a real Princess and no question about it, now that she had felt one pea all the way through twenty mattresses and twenty more feather beds. Nobody but a Princess could be so delicate. So the Prince made haste to marry her, because he knew he had found a real Princess.

As for the pea, they put it in the museum. There it's still to be seen, unless somebody has taken it.

There, that's a true story.

The Nightingale

The Emperor of China is a Chinaman, as you most likely know, and everyone around him is a Chinaman too. It's been a great many years since this story happened in China, but that's all the more reason for telling it before it gets forgotten.

The Emperor's palace was the wonder of the world. It was made entirely of fine porcelain, extremely expensive but so delicate that you could touch it only with the greatest of care. In the garden the rarest flowers bloomed, and to the prettiest ones were tied little silver bells which tinkled so that no one could pass by without noticing them. Yes, all things were arranged according to plan in the Emperor's garden, though how far and wide it extended not even the gardener knew. If you walked on and on, you came to a fine forest where the trees were tall and the lakes were deep. The forest ran down to the deep blue sea, so close that tall ships could sail under the branches of the trees. In these trees a nightingale lived. His song was so ravishing that even the poor fisherman, who had much else to do, stopped to listen on the nights when he went out to cast his nets, and heard the nightingale.

»How beautiful that is,« he said, but he had his work to attend to, and he would forget the bird's song. But the next night, when he heard the song he would again say, »How beautiful.«

From all the countries in the world travelers came to the city of the Emperor. They admired the city. They admired the palace and its garden, but when they heard the nightingale they said, »That is the best of all.«

And the travelers told of it when they came home, and men of learning wrote many books about the town, about the palace, and about the garden. But they did not forget the nightingale. They praised him highest of all, and those who were poets wrote magnificent poems about the nightingale who lived in the forest by the deep sea.

These books went all the world over, and some of them came even to the Emperor of China. He sat in his golden chair and read, and read, nodding his head in delight over such glowing descriptions of his city, and palace, and garden. *But the nightingale is the best of all.* He read it in print.

»What's this?« the Emperor exclaimed. »I don't know of any nightingale. Can there be such a bird in my empire – in my own garden – and I not know it? To think that I should have to learn of it out of a book.«

Thereupon he called his Lord-in-Waiting, who was so exalted that when anyone of lower rank dared speak to him, or ask him a question, he only answered, »P,« which means nothing at all.

»They say there's a most remarkable bird called the nightingale,« said the Emperor. »They say it's the best thing in all my empire. Why haven't I been told about it?«

»I've never heard the name mentioned,« said the Lord-in-Waiting. »He hasn't been presented at court.«

»I command that he appear before me this evening, and sing,« said the Emperor. »The whole world knows my possessions better than I do!«

»I never heard of him before,« said the Lord-in-Waiting. »But I shall look for him. I'll find him.«

But where? The Lord-in-Waiting ran upstairs and downstairs, through all the rooms and corridors, but no one he met with had ever heard tell of the nightingale. So the Lord-in-Waiting ran back to the Emperor, and said it must be a story invented by those who write books. »Your Imperial Majesty would scarcely believe how much of what is written is fiction, if not downright black art.«

»But the book I read was sent me by the mighty Emperor of Japan,« said the Emperor. »Therefore it can't be a pack of lies. I must hear this nightingale. I insist upon his being here this evening. He has my high imperial favor, and if he is not forthcoming I will have the whole court punched in the stomach, directly after supper.«

»Tsing-pe!« said the Lord-in-Waiting, and off he scurried up the stairs, through all the rooms and corridors. And half the court ran with him, for no one wanted to be punched in the stomach after supper.

There was much questioning as to the whereabouts of this remarkable nightingale, who was so well known everywhere in the world except at home. At last they found a poor little kitchen girl, who said:

»The nightingale? I know him well. Yes, indeed he can sing. Every evening I get leave to carry scraps from table to my sick mother. She lives down by the shore. When I start back I am tired, and rest in the woods. Then I hear the nightingale sing. It brings tears to my eyes. It's as if my mother were kissing me.«

»Little kitchen girl,« said the Lord-in-Waiting, »I'll have you appointed scullion for life. I'll even get permission for you to watch the Emperor dine, if you'll take us to the nightingale who is commanded to appear at court this evening.«

So they went into the forest where the nightingale usually sang. Half the court went along. On the way to the forest a cow began to moo.

»Oh,« cried a courtier, »that must be it. What a powerful voice for a creature so small. I'm sure I've heard her sing before.«

»No, that's the cow lowing,« said the little kitchen girl. »We still have a long way to go.«

Then the frogs in the marsh began to croak.

»Glorious!« said the Chinese court parson. »Now I hear it – like church bells ringing.«

»No, that's the frogs,« said the little kitchen girl. »But I think we shall hear him soon.«

41

Then the nightingale sang.

»That's it,« said the little kitchen girl. »Listen, listen! And yonder he sits.« She pointed to a little gray bird high up in the branches.

»Is it possible?« cried the Lord-in-Waiting. »Well, I never would have thought he looked like that, so unassuming. But he has probably turned pale at seeing so many important people around him.«

»Little nightingale,« the kitchen girl called to him, »our gracious Emperor wants to hear you sing.«

»With the greatest of pleasure,« answered the nightingale, and burst into song.

»Very similar to the sound of glass bells,« said the Lord-in-Waiting. »Just see his little throat, how busily it throbs. I'm astounded that we have never heard him before. I'm sure he'll be a great success at court.«

»Shall I sing to the Emperor again?« asked the nightingale, for he thought that the Emperor was present.

»My good little nightingale,« said the Lord-in-Waiting, »I have the honour to command your presence at a court function this evening, where you'll delight His Majesty the Emperor with your charming song.«

»My song sounds best in the woods,« said the nightingale, but he went with them willingly when he heard it was the Emperor's wish.

The palace had been especially polished for the occasion. The porcelain walls and floors shone in the rays of many gold lamps. The flowers with tinkling bells on them had been brought into the halls, and there was such a commotion of coming and going that all the bells chimed away until you could scarcely hear yourself talk.

In the middle of the great throne room, where the Emperor sat, there was a golden perch for the nightingale. The whole court was there, and they let the little kitchen girl stand behind the door, now that she had been appointed »Imperial Pot-Walloper.« Everyone was dressed in his best, and all stared at the little gray bird to which the Emperor graciously nodded.

And the nightingale sang so sweetly that tears came into the Emperor's

eyes and rolled down his cheeks. Then the nightingale sang still more sweetly, and it was the Emperor's heart that melted. The Emperor was so touched that he wanted his own golden slipper hung round the nightingale's neck, but the nightingale declined it with thanks. He had already been amply rewarded.

»I have seen tears in the Emperor's eyes,« he said. »Nothing could surpass that. An Emperor's tears are strangely powerful. I have my reward.« And he sang again, gloriously.

»It's the most charming coquetry we ever heard,« said the ladies-in-waiting. And they took water in their mouths so they could gurgle when anyone spoke to them, hoping to rival the nightingale. Even the lackeys and chambermaids said they were satisfied, which was saying a great deal, for they were the hardest to please. Unquestionably the nightingale was a success. He was to stay at court, and have his own cage. He had permission to go for a walk twice a day, and once a night. Twelve footmen attended him, each one holding tight to a ribbon tied to the bird's leg. There wasn't much fun in such outings.

The whole town talked about the marvelous bird, and if two people met, one could scarcely say »night« before the other said »gale,« and then they would sigh in unison, with no need for words. Eleven pork-butchers' children were named »Nightingale,« but not one could sing.

One day the Emperor received a large package labeled »The Nightingale.«

»This must be another book about my celebrated bird,« he said. But it was not a book. In the box was a work of art, an artificial nightingale most like the real one except that it was encrusted with diamonds, rubies and sapphires. When it was wound, the artificial bird could sing one of the nightingale's songs while it wagged its glittering gold and silver tail. Round its neck hung a ribbon inscribed: »The Emperor of Japan's nightingale is a poor thing compared with that of the Emperor of China.«

»Isn't that nice?« everyone said, and the man who had brought the contraption was immediately promoted to be »Imperial-Nightingale-Fetcher-in-Chief.«

»Now let's have them sing together. What a duet that will be,« said the courtiers.

So they had to sing together, but it didn't turn out so well, for the real nightingale sang whatever came into his head while the imitation bird sang by rote.

»That's not the newcomer's fault,« said the music master. »He keeps perfect time, just as I have taught him.«

Then they had the imitation bird sing by itself. It met with the same success as the real nightingale, and besides it was much prettier to see, all sparkling like bracelets and breastpins. Three and thirty times it sang the selfsame song without tiring. The courtiers would gladly have heard it again, but the Emperor said the real nightingale should now have his turn. Where was he? No one had noticed him flying out the open window, back to his home in the green forest.

»But what made him do that?« said the Emperor.

All the courtiers slandered the nightingale, whom they called a most un-grateful wretch. »Luckily we have the best bird,« they said, and made the imita-tion one sing again. That was the thirty-fourth time they had heard the same tune, but they didn't quite know it by heart because it was a difficult piece. And the music master praised the artificial bird beyond measure. Yes, he said that the contraption was much better than the real nightingale, not only in its dress and its many beautiful diamonds, but also in its mechanical interior.

»You see, ladies and gentlemen, and above all Your Imperial Majesty, with a real nightingale one never knows what to expect, but with this artificial bird everything goes according to plan. Nothing is left to chance. I can explain it and take it to pieces, and show how the mechanical wheels are arranged, how they go around, and how one follows after another.«

»Those are our sentiments exactly,« said they all, and the music master was commanded to have the bird give a public concert next Sunday. The Emperor said that his people should hear it. And hear it they did, with as much pleasure as if they had all got tipsy on tea, Chinese fashion. Everyone said, »Oh,« and held up the finger we call »lickpot«, and nodded his head. But the poor fishermen who had heard the real nightingale said, »This is very pretty, very nearly the real thing, but not quite. I can't imagine what's lacking.«

The real nightingale had been banished from the land. In its place, the artificial bird sat on a cushion beside the Emperor's bed. All its gold and jewelled presents lay about it, and its title was now »Grand Imperial Singer-of-the-Emperor-to-Sleep.« In rank it stood first from the left, for the Emperor gave preeminence to the left side because of the heart. Even an Emperor's heart is on the left.

The music master wrote a twenty-five-volume book about the artificial bird. It was learned, long-winded, and full of hard Chinese words, yet everybody said they had read and understood it, lest they show themselves stupid and would then have been punched in their stomachs.

After a year the Emperor, his court, and all the other Chinamen knew every twitter of the artificial song by heart. They liked it all the better now that they could sing it themselves. Which they did. The street urchins sang, »Zizizi! kluk, kluk, kluk,« and the Emperor sang it too. That's how popular it was.

But one night, while the artificial bird was singing his best by the

Emperor's bed, something inside the bird broke with a twang. *Whir-r-r*, all the wheels ran down and the music stopped. Out of bed jumped the Emperor and sent for his own physician, but what could he do? Then he sent for a watchmaker, who conferred, and investigated, and patched up the bird after a fashion. But the watchmaker said that the bird must be spared too much exertion, for the cogs were badly worn and if he replaced them it would spoil the tune. This was terrible. Only once a year could they let the bird sing, and that was almost too much for it. But the music master made a little speech full of hard Chinese words which meant that the bird was as good as it ever was. So that made it as good as ever.

Five years passed by, and a real sorrow befell the whole country. The Chinamen loved their Emperor, and now he fell ill. Ill unto death, it was said. A new Emperor was chosen in readiness. People stood in the palace street and asked the Lord-in-Waiting how it went with their Emperor.

»P,« said he, and shook his head.

Cold and pale lay the Emperor in his great magnificent bed. All the courtiers thought he was dead, and went to do homage to the new Emperor. The lackeys went off to trade gossip, and the chambermaids gave a coffee party because it was such a special occasion. Deep mats were laid in all the rooms and passageways, to muffle each footstep. It was quiet in the palace, dead quiet. But the Emperor was not yet dead. Stiff and pale he lay, in his magnificent bed with the long velvet curtains and the heavy gold tassels. High in the wall was an open window, through which moonlight fell on the Emperor and his artificial bird.

The poor Emperor could hardly breathe. It was as if something were sitting on his chest. Opening his eyes he saw it was Death who sat there, wearing the Emperor's crown, handling the Emperor's gold sword, and carrying the Emperor's silk banner. Among the folds of the great velvet curtains there were strangely familiar faces. Some were horrible, others gentle and kind. They were the Emperor's deeds, good and bad, who came back to him now that Death sat on his heart.

»Don't you remember –?« they whispered one after the other. »Don't you remember –?« And they told him of things that made the cold sweat run on his forehead.

»No, I will not remember!« said the Emperor. »Music, music, sound the great drum of China lest I hear what they say!« But they went on whispering, and Death nodded, Chinese fashion, at every word.

»Music, music!« the Emperor called. »Sing, my precious little golden bird, sing! I have given you gold and precious presents. I have hung my golden slipper around your neck. Sing, I pray you, sing!«

But the bird stood silent. There was no one to wind it, nothing to make it sing. Death kept staring through his great hollow eyes, and it was quiet, deadly quiet.

Suddenly, through the window came a burst of song. It was the little live nightingale who sat outside on a spray. He had heard of the Emperor's plight, and had come to sing of comfort and hope. As he sang, the phantoms grew pale, and still more pale, and the blood flowed quicker and quicker through the Emperor's feeble body. Even Death listened, and said. »Go on, little nightingale, go on!«

»But,« said the little nightingale, »will you give back that sword, that banner, that Emperor's crown?«

And Death gave back these treasures for a song. The nightingale sang on. It sang of the quiet churchyard where white roses grow, where the elder flowers make the air sweet, and where the grass is always green, wet with the tears of those who are still alive. Death longed for his garden. Out through the windows drifted a cold gray mist, as Death departed.

»Thank you, thank you!« the Emperor said. »Little bird from Heaven, I know you of old. I banished you once from my land, and yet you have sung away the evil faces from my bed, and Death from my heart. How can I repay you?«

»You have already rewarded me,« said the nightingale. »I brought tears to your eyes when first I sang for you. To the heart of a singer those are more

precious than any precious stone. But sleep now, and grow fresh and strong while I sing.« He sang on until the Emperor fell into a sound, refreshing sleep, a sweet and soothing slumber.

The sun was shining in his window when the Emperor awoke, restored and well. Not one of his servants had returned to him, for they thought him dead, but the nightingale still sang.

»You must stay with me always,« said the Emperor. »Sing to me only when you please. I shall break the artificial bird into a thousand pieces.«

»No,« said the nightingale. »It did its best. Keep it near you. I cannot build my nest here, or live in a palace, so let me come as I will. Then I shall sit on the spray by your window, and sing things that will make you happy and thoughtful too. I'll sing about those who are gay, and those who are sorrowful.

My songs will tell you of all the good and evil that you do not see. A little singing bird flies far and wide, to the fisherman's hut, to the farmer's home, and to many other places a long way off from you and your court. I love your heart better than I do your crown, and yet the crown has been blessed too. I will come and sing to you, if you will promise me one thing.«

»All that I have is yours,« cried the Emperor, who stood in his imperial robes, which he had put on himself, and held his heavy gold sword to his heart.

»One thing only,« the nightingale asked. »You must not let anyone know that you have a little bird who tells you everything; then all will go even better.« And away he flew.

The servants came in to look after their dead Emperor – and there they stood. And the Emperor said, »Good morning.«

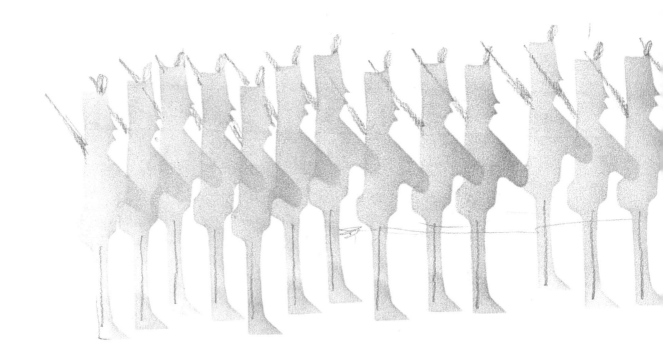

The Steadfast Tin Soldier

There were once five-and-twenty tin soldiers. They were all brothers, born of the same old tin spoon. They shouldered their muskets and looked straight ahead of them, splendid in their uniforms, all red and blue.

The very first thing in the world that they heard was, »Tin soldiers!« A small boy shouted it and clapped his hands as the lid was lifted off their box on his birthday. He immediately set them up on the table.

All the soldiers looked exactly alike except one. He looked a little different as he had been cast last of all. The tin was short, so he had only one leg. But

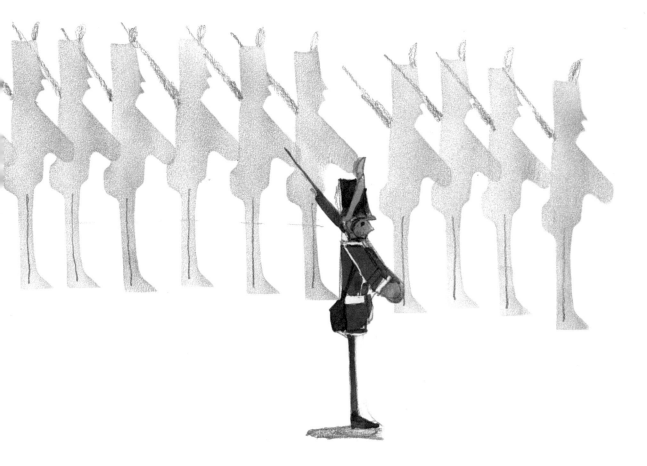

there he stood, as steady on one leg as any of the other soldiers on their two. But just you see, he'll be the remarkable one.

On the table with the soldiers were many other playthings, and one that no eye could miss was a marvellous castle of cardboard. It had little windows through which you could look right inside it. And in front of the castle were miniature trees around a little mirror supposed to represent a lake. The wax swans that swam on its surface were reflected in the mirror. All this was very pretty but prettiest of all was the little lady who stood in the open doorway of the castle. Though she was a paper doll, she wore a dress of the fluffiest gauze. A tiny blue ribbon went over her shoulder for a scarf, and in the middle of it shone a spangle that was as big as her face. The little lady held out both her arms, as a ballet dancer does, and one leg was lifted so high behind her that the tin soldier couldn't see it at all, and he supposed she must have only one leg, as he did.

»That would be a wife for me,« he thought. »But maybe she's too grand. She lives in a castle. I have only a box, with four-and-twenty roommates to share it. That's no place for her. But I must try to make her acquaintance.« Still as stiff as when he stood at attention, he lay down on the table behind a snuffbox, where he could admire the dainty little dancer who kept standing on one leg without ever losing her balance.

When the evening came the other tin soldiers were put away in their box, and the people of the house went to bed. Now the toys began to play among themselves at visits, and battles, and at giving balls. The tin soldiers rattled about in their box, for they wanted to play too, but they could not get the lid open. The nutcracker turned somersaults, and the slate pencil squeaked out jokes on the slate. The toys made such a noise that they woke up the canary bird, who made them a speech, all in verse. The only two who stayed still were the tin soldier and the little dancer. Without ever swerving from the tip of one toe, she held out her arms to him, and the tin soldier was just as steadfast on his one leg. Not once did he take his eyes off her.

Then the clock struck twelve and – *clack!* – up popped the lid of the snuffbox. But there was no snuff in it, no – out bounced a little black bogey, a jack-in-the-box.

»Tin soldier,« he said. »Will you please keep your eyes to yourself?«

The tin soldier pretended not to hear.

The bogey said, »Just you wait till tomorrow.«

But when morning came, and the children got up, the soldier was set on the window ledge. And whether the bogey did it, or there was a gust of wind, all of a sudden the window flew open and the soldier pitched out headlong from the third floor. He fell at breathtaking speed and landed cap first, with his bayonet buried between the paving stones and his one leg stuck straight in the air. The housemaid and the little boy ran down to look for him and,

though they nearly stepped on the tin soldier, they walked right past without seeing him. If the soldier had called, »Here I am!« they would surely have found him, but he thought it contemptible to raise an uproar while he was wearing his uniform.

Soon it began to rain. The drops fell faster and faster, until they came down by the bucketful. As soon as the rain let up, along came two young rapscallions.

»Hi, look!« one of them said, »there's a tin soldier. Let's send him sailing.«

They made a boat out of newspaper, put the tin soldier in the middle of it, and away he went down the gutter with the two young rapscallions running beside him and clapping their hands. High heavens! How the waves splashed, and how fast the water ran down the gutter. Don't forget that it had just been raining by the bucketful. The paper boat pitched, and tossed, and sometimes it whirled about so rapidly that it made the soldier's head spin. But he stood as steady as ever. Never once flinching, he kept his eyes front, and carried his gun shoulder-high. Suddenly the boat rushed under a long plank where the gutter was boarded over. It was as dark as the soldier's own box.

»Where can I be going?« the soldier wondered. »This must be that black bogey's revenge. Ah! if only I had the little lady with me, it could be twice as dark here for all that I would care.«

Out popped a great water rat who lived under the gutter plank.

»Have you a passport?« said the rat. »Hand it over.«

The soldier kept quiet and held his musket tighter. On rushed the boat, and the rat came right after it, gnashing his teeth as he called to the sticks and straws:

»Halt him! Stop him! He didn't pay his toll. He hasn't shown his passport.«

But the current ran stronger and stronger. The soldier could see daylight ahead where the board ended, but he also heard a roar that would frighten the bravest of us. Hold on! Right at the end of that gutter plank the water poured into the great canal. It was as dangerous to him as a waterfall would be to us.

He was so near it he could not possibly stop. The boat plunged into the whirlpool. The poor tin soldier stood as staunch as he could, and no one can say that he so much as blinked an eye. Thrice and again the boat spun around. It filled to the top and was bound to sink. The water was up to his neck and still the boat went down, deeper, deeper, deeper, and the paper got soft and limp. Then the water rushed over his head. He thought of the pretty little dancer whom he'd never see again, and in his ears rang an old, old song:

>»Farewell, farewell, O warrior brave,
>Nobody can from Death thee save.«

And now the paper boat broke beneath the soldier, and he sank right through. And just at that moment he was swallowed by a most enormous fish.

My! how dark it was inside that fish. It was darker than under the gutter-plank and it was so cramped, but the tin soldier still was staunch. He lay there full length, soldier fashion, with musket to shoulder.

Then the fish flopped and floundered in a most unaccountable way. Finally it was perfectly still, and after a while something struck through him like a flash of lightning. The tin soldier saw daylight again, and he heard a voice say, »A Tin Soldier!« The fish had been caught, carried to market, bought, and brought to a kitchen where the cook cut him open with her big knife.

She picked the soldier up bodily between her two fingers, and carried him off upstairs. Everyone wanted to see this remarkable traveler who had traveled about in a fish's stomach, but the tin soldier took no pride in it. They put

him on the table and – lo and behold, what curious things can happen in this world – there he was, back in the same room as before. He saw the same children, the same toys were on the table, and there was the same fine castle with the pretty little dancer. She still balanced on one leg, with the other raised high. She too was steadfast. That touched the soldier so deeply that he

would have cried tin tears, only soldiers never cry. He looked at her, and she looked at him, and never a word was said. Just as things were going so nicely for them, one of the little boys snatched up the tin soldier and threw him into the stove. He did it for no reason at all. That black bogey in the snuffbox must have put him up to it.

The tin soldier stood there dressed in flames. He felt a terrible heat, but whether it came from the flames or from his love he didn't know. He'd lost his splendid colours, maybe from his hard journey, maybe from grief, nobody can say.

He looked at the little lady, and she looked at him, and he felt himself melting. But still he stood steadfast, with his musket held trim on his shoulder.

Then the door blew open. A puff of wind struck the dancer. She flew like a sylph, straight into the fire with the soldier, blazed up in a flash, and was gone. The tin soldier melted, all in a lump. The next day, when a servant took up the ashes she found him in the shape of a little tin heart. But of the pretty dancer nothing was left except her spangle, and that was burned as black as a coal.

The Emperor's
New Clothes

Many years ago there was an Emperor so exceedingly fond of new clothes that he spent all his money on being well dressed. He cared nothing about reviewing his soldiers, going to the theatre, or going for a ride in his carriage, except to show off his new clothes. He had a coat for every hour of the day, and instead of saying, as one might, about any other ruler, »The King's in council,« here they always said, »The Emperor's in his dressing room.«

In the great city where he lived, life was always gay. Every day many strangers came to town, and among them one day came two swindlers. They let it be known they were weavers, and they said they could weave the most magnificent fabrics imaginable. Not only were their colours and patterns uncommonly fine, but clothes made of this cloth had a wonderful way of becoming invisible to anyone who was unfit for his office, or who was unusually stupid.

»Those would be just the clothes for me,« thought the Emperor. »If I wore them I would be able to discover which men in my empire are unfit for their posts. And I could tell the wise men from the fools. Yes, I certainly must get some of the stuff woven for me right away.« He paid the two swindlers a large sum of money to start work at once.

They set up two looms and pretended to weave, though there was nothing on the looms. All the finest silk and the purest old thread which they demanded went into their travelling bags, while they worked the empty looms far into the night.

»I'd like to know how those weavers are getting on with the cloth,« the Emperor thought, but he felt slightly uncomfortable when he remembered that those who were unfit for their position would not be able to see the fabric. It couldn't have been that he doubted himself, yet he thought he'd rather send someone else to see how things were going. The whole town knew about the cloth's peculiar power, and all were impatient to find out how stupid their neighbours were.

»I'll send my honest old minister to the weavers,« the Emperor decided. »He'll be the best one to tell me how the material looks, for he's a sensible man and no one does his duty better.«

So the honest old minister went to the room where the two swindlers sat working away at their empty looms.

»Heaven help me,« he thought as his eyes flew wide open, »I can't see anything at all.« But he did not say so.

Both the swindlers begged him to be so kind as to come near to approve the excellent pattern, the beautiful colours. They pointed to the empty looms, and the poor old minister stared as hard as he dared. He couldn't see anything, because there was nothing to see. »Heaven have mercy,« he thought. »Can it be that I'm a fool? I'd have never guessed it, and not a soul must know. Am I unfit to be the minister? It would never do to let on that I can't see the cloth.«

»Don't hesitate to tell us what you think of it,« said one of the weavers.

»Oh, it's beautiful – it's enchanting.« The old minister peered through his spectacles. »Such a pattern, what colours! I'll be sure to tell the Emperor how delighted I am with it.«

»We're pleased to hear that,« the swindlers said. They proceeded to name all the colours and to explain the intricate pattern. The old minister paid the closest attention, so that he could tell it all to the Emperor. And so he did.

The swindlers at once asked for more money, more silk and gold thread, to get on with the weaving. But it all went into their pockets. Not a thread went into the looms, though they worked at their weaving as hard as ever.

The Emperor presently sent another trustworthy official to see how the work progressed and how soon it would be ready. The same thing happened to him that had happened to the minister. He looked and he looked, but as there was nothing to see in the looms he couldn't see anything.

»Isn't it a beautiful piece of goods?« the swindlers asked him, as they displayed and described their imaginary pattern.

»I know I'm not stupid,« the man thought, »so it must be that I'm unworthy of my good office. That's strange. I mustn't let anyone find it out, though.« So he praised the material he did not see. He declared he was delighted with the beautiful colours and the exquisite pattern. To the Emperor he said, »It held me spellbound.«

All the town was talking of this splendid cloth, and the Emperor wanted to see it for himself while it was still in the looms. Attended by a band of chosen men, among whom were his two old trusted officials – the ones who had been to the weavers – he set out to see the two swindlers. He found them weaving with might and main, but without a thread in their looms.

»Magnificent,« said the two officials already duped. »Just look, Your Majesty, what colours! What a design!« They pointed to the empty looms, each supposing that the others could see the stuff.

»What's this?« thought the Emperor. »I can't see anything. This is terrible! Am I a fool? Am I unfit to be the Emperor? What a thing to happen to me of all people! – Oh! it's *very* pretty,« he said. »It has my highest approval.« And he nodded approbation at the empty loom. Nothing could make him say that he couldn't see anything.

His whole retinue stared and stared. One saw no more than another, but they all joined the Emperor in exclaiming, »Oh! It's *very* pretty,« and they advised him to wear clothes made of this wonderful cloth especially for the great procession he was soon to lead. »Magnificent! Excellent! Unsurpassed!«

62

were bandied from mouth to mouth, and everyone did his best to seem well pleased. The Emperor gave each of the swindlers a cross to wear in his button-hole, and the title of »Sir Weaver.«

Before the procession the swindlers sat up all night and burned more than sixteen candles, to show how busy they were finishing the Emperor's new clothes. They pretended to take the cloth off the loom. They made cuts in the air with huge scissors. And at last they said, »Now the Emperor's new clothes are ready for him.«

Then the Emperor himself came with his noblest noblemen, and the swindlers each raised an arm as if they were holding something. They said, »There are the trousers, here's the coat, and this is the mantle,« naming each garment. »All of them are as light as a spider web. One would almost think he had nothing on, but that's what makes them so fine.«

»Exactly,« all the noblemen agreed, though they could see nothing, for there was nothing to see.

»If Your Imperial Majesty will condescend to take your clothes off,« said the swindlers, »we will help you on with your new ones here in front of the long mirror.«

The Emperor undressed, and the swindlers pretended to put his new clothes on him, one garment after another. They took him around the waist and seemed to be fastening something – that was his train – as the Emperor turned round and round before the looking glass.

»How well Your Majesty's new clothes look. Aren't they becoming!« He heard on all sides, »That pattern, so perfect! Those colours, so suitable! It is a magnificent outfit.«

Then the minister of public processions announced, »Your Majesty's canopy is waiting outside.«

»Well, I'm supposed to be ready,« the Emperor said, and turned again for one last look in the mirror. »It is a remarkable fit, isn't it?« He seemed to regard his costume with the greatest interest.

The noblemen who were to carry his train stooped low and reached for the floor as if they were picking up his mantle. Then they pretended to lift and hold it high. They didn't dare admit they had nothing to hold.

So off went the Emperor in procession under his splendid canopy. Everyone in the streets and the windows said, »Oh, how fine are the Emperor's new clothes! Don't they fit him to perfection? And see his long train!« Nobody would confess that he couldn't see anything, for that would prove him either unfit for his position, or a fool. No costume the Emperor had worn before was ever such a complete success.

»But he hasn't got anything on,« a little child said.

»Did you ever hear such innocent prattle?« said its father. And one person whispered to another what the child had said, »He hasn't anything on. A child says he hasn't anything on.«

»But he hasn't got anything on!« the whole town cried out at last.

The Emperor shivered, for he suspected they were right. But he thought, »This procession has got to go on.« So he walked more proudly than ever, as his noblemen held high the train that wasn't there at all.

The Ugly Duckling

It was so beautiful out in the country, it was summer – the wheat fields were golden, the oats were green, and down among the green meadows the hay was stacked. There the stork minced about on his red legs, clacking away in Egyptian, which was the language his mother had taught him. Round about the field and meadow lands rose vast forests, in which deep lakes lay hidden. Yes, it was indeed lovely out there in the country.

In the midst of the sunshine there stood an old manor house that had a deep moat around it. From the walls of the manor right down to the water's edge great burdock leaves grew, and there were some so tall that little children could stand upright beneath the biggest of them. In this wilderness of leaves, which was as dense as the forest itself, a duck sat on her nest, hatching her ducklings. She was becoming somewhat weary, because sitting is such a dull business and scarcely anyone came to see her. The other ducks would much rather swim in the moat than waddle out and squat under a burdock leaf to gossip with her.

But at last the eggshells began to crack, one after another. »Peep, peep!« said the little things, as they came to life and poked out their heads.

»Quack, quack!« said the duck, and quick as quick can be they all waddled out to have a look at the green world under the leaves. Their mother let them look as much as they pleased, because green is good for the eyes.

»How wide the world is,« said all the young ducks, for they certainly had much more room now than they had when they were in their eggshells.

»Do you think this is the whole world?« their mother asked. »Why, it extends on and on, clear across to the other side of the garden and right on into the parson's field, though that is further than I have ever been. I do hope

66

you are all hatched,« she said as she got up. »No, not quite all. The biggest egg still lies here. How much longer is this going to take? I am really rather tired of it all,« she said, but she settled back on her nest.

»Well, how goes it?« asked an old duck who came to pay her a call.

»It takes a long time with that one egg,« said the duck on the nest. »It won't crack, but look at the others. They are the cutest little ducklings I've ever seen. They look exactly like their father, the wretch! he hasn't come to see me at all.«

»Let's have a look at the egg that won't crack,« the old duck said. »It's a turkey egg, and you can take my word for it. I was fooled like that once myself. What trouble and care I had with those turkey children, for I may as well tell you, they are afraid of the water. I simply could not get them into it. I quacked and snapped at them, but it wasn't a bit of use. Let me see the egg. Certainly, it's a turkey egg. Let it lie, and go teach your other children to swim.«

»Oh, I'll sit a little longer. I've been at it so long already that I may as well sit here half the summer.«

»Suit yourself,« said the old duck, and away she waddled.

At last the big egg did crack. »Peep,« said the young one, and out he tumbled, but he was so big and ugly.

The duck took a look at him. »That's a frightfully big duckling,« she said. »He doesn't look the least like the others. Can he really be a turkey baby? Well, well! I'll soon find out. Into the water he shall go, even if I have to shove him in myself.«

Next day the weather was perfectly splendid, and the sun shone down on all the green burdock leaves. The mother duck led her whole family down to the moat. Splash! she took to the water. »Quack, quack,« said she, and one duckling after another plunged in. The water went over their heads, but they came up in a flash, and floated to perfection. Their legs worked automatically, and they were all there in the water. Even the big, ugly gray one was swimming along.

»Why, that's no turkey,« she said. »See how nicely he uses his legs, and how straight he holds himself. He's my very own son after all, and quite good-looking if you look at him properly. Quack, quack, come with me. I'll lead you out into the world and introduce you to the duck yard. But keep close to me so that you won't get stepped on, and watch out for the cat!«

Thus they sallied into the duck yard, where all was in an uproar because two families were fighting over the head of an eel. But the cat got it, after all.

»You see, that's the way of the world.« The mother duck licked her bill because she wanted the eel's head for herself. »Stir your legs. Bustle about, and mind that you bend your necks to that old duck over there. She's the noblest of us all, and has Spanish blood in her. That's why she's so fat. See that red rag around her leg? That's a wonderful thing, and the highest distinction a duck can get. It shows that they don't want to lose her, and that she's to have special attention from man and beast. Shake yourselves! Don't turn your toes in. A well-bred duckling turns his toes way out, just as his father and mother do – this way. So then! Now duck your necks and say quack!«

They did as she told them, but the other ducks around them looked on and said right out loud, »See here! Must we have this brood too, just as if there weren't enough of us already? And – fie! what an ugly-looking fellow that duckling is! We won't stand for him.« One duck charged up and bit his neck.

»Let him alone,« his mother said. »He isn't doing any harm.«

»Possibly not,« said the duck who bit him, »but he's too big and strange, and therefore he needs a good whacking.«

»What nice-looking children you have, Mother,« said the old duck with the rag around her leg. »They are all pretty except that one. He didn't come out so well. It's a pity you can't hatch him again.«

»That can't be managed, your ladyship,« said the mother. »He isn't so handsome, but he's as good as can be, and he swims just as well as the rest, or, I should say, even a little better than they do. I hope his looks will improve with age, and after a while he won't seem so big. He took too long in the egg, and that's why his figure isn't all that it should be.« She pinched his neck and preened his feathers. »Moreover, he's a drake, so it won't matter so much. I think he will be quite strong, and I'm sure he will amount to something.«

»The other ducklings are pretty enough,« said the old duck. »Now make yourselves right at home, and if you find an eel's head you may bring it to me.«

So they felt quite at home. But the poor duckling, who had been the last one out of his egg, and who looked so ugly, was pecked and pushed about and made fun of by the ducks, and the chickens as well. »He's too big,« said they all. The turkey gobbler, who thought himself an emperor because he was born wearing spurs, puffed up like a ship under full sail and bore down upon him, gobbling and gobbling until he was red in the face. The poor duckling did not know where he dared stand or where he dared walk. He was so sad because he was so desperately ugly, and because he was the laughing stock of the whole barnyard.

So it went on the first day, and after that things went from bad to worse. The poor duckling was chased and buffeted about by everyone. Even his own brothers and sisters abused him. »Oh,« they would always say, »how we wish the cat would catch you, you ugly thing.« And his mother said, »How I do wish you were miles away.« The ducks nipped him, and the hens pecked him, and the girl who fed them kicked him with her foot.

So he ran away; and he flew over the fence. The little birds in the bushes darted up in a fright. »That's because I'm so ugly,« he thought, and closed his eyes, but he ran on just the same until he reached the great marsh where the wild ducks lived. There he lay all night long, weary and disheartened.

When morning came, the wild ducks flew up to have a look at their new companion. »What sort of creature are you?« they asked, as the duckling turned in all directions, bowing his best to them all. »You are terribly ugly,« they told him, »but that's nothing to us so long as you don't marry into our family.«

Poor duckling! Marriage certainly had never entered his mind. All he wanted was for them to let him lie among the reeds and drink a little water from the marsh.

There he stayed for two whole days. Then he met two wild geese, or rather

wild ganders – for they were males. They had not been out of the shell very long, and that's what made them so sure of themselves.

»Say there, comrade,« they said, »you're so ugly that we have taken a fancy to you. Come with us and be a bird of passage. In another marsh near-by, there are some fetching wild geese, all nice young ladies who know how to quack. You are so ugly that you'll completely turn their heads.«

Bing! Bang! Shots rang in the air, and these two ganders fell dead among the reeds. The water was red with their blood. Bing! Bang! the shots rang, and as whole flocks of wild geese flew up from the reeds another volley crashed. A great hunt was in progress. The hunters lay under cover all around the marsh, and some even perched on branches of trees that overhung the reeds.

Blue smoke rose like clouds from the shade of the trees, and drifted far out over the water.

The bird dogs came splash, splash! through the swamp, bending down the reeds and the rushes on every side. This gave the poor duckling such a fright that he twisted his head about to hide it under his wing. But at that very moment a fearfully big dog appeared right beside him. His tongue lolled out of his mouth and his wicked eyes glared horribly. He opened his wide jaws, flashed his sharp teeth, and – *splash, splash* – on he went without touching the duckling.

»Thank heavens,« he sighed, »I'm so ugly that the dog won't even bother to bite me.«

He lay perfectly still, while the bullets splattered through the reeds as shot after shot was fired. It was late in the day before things became quiet again, and even then the poor duckling didn't dare move. He waited several hours before he ventured to look about him, and then he scurried away from that marsh as fast as he could go. He ran across field and meadows. The wind was so strong that he had to struggle to keep his feet.

Late in the evening he came to a miserable little hovel, so ramshackle that it did not know which way to tumble, and that was the only reason it still stood. The wind struck the duckling so hard that the poor little fellow had to sit down on his tail to withstand it. The storm blew stronger and stronger, but the duckling noticed that one hinge had come loose and the door hung so crooked that he could squeeze through the crack into the room, and that's just what he did.

Here lived an old woman with her cat and her hen. The cat, whom she called »Sonny«, could arch his back, purr, and even make sparks, though for that you had to stroke his fur the wrong way. The hen had short little legs, so she was called »Chickey Shortleg«. She laid good eggs, and the old woman loved her as if she had been her own child.

In the morning they were quick to notice the strange duckling. The cat began to purr, and the hen began to cluck.

»What on earth!« The old woman looked around, but she was short-sighted, and she mistook the duckling for a fat duck that had lost its way. »That was a good catch,« she said. »Now I shall have duck eggs – unless it's a drake. We must try it out.« So the duckling was tried out for three weeks, but not one egg did he lay.

In this house the cat was master and the hen was mistress. They always said, »We and the world,« for they thought themselves half of the world, and much the better half at that. The duckling thought that there might be more than one way of thinking, but the hen would not hear of it.

»Can you lay eggs?« she asked.

»No.«

»Then be so good as to hold your tongue.«

The cat asked, »Can you arch your back, purr, or make sparks?«

»No.«

»Then keep your opinion to yourself when sensible people are talking.«

The duckling sat in a corner, feeling most despondent. Then he remembered the fresh air and the sunlight. Such a desire to go swimming on the water possessed him that he could not help telling the hen about it.

»What on earth has come over you?« the hen cried. »You haven't a thing to

do, and that's why you get such silly notions. Lay us an egg, or learn to purr, and you'll get over it.«

»But it's so refreshing to float on the water,« said the duckling, »so refreshing to feel it rise over your head as you dive to the bottom.«

»Yes, it must be a great pleasure!« said the hen. »I think you must have gone crazy. Ask the cat, who's the wisest fellow I know, whether he likes to swim or dive down in the water. Of myself I say nothing. But ask the old woman, our mistress. There's no one on earth wiser than she is. Do you imagine she wants to go swimming and feel the water rise over her head?«

»You don't understand me,« said the duckling.

»Well, if we don't, who would? Surely you don't think you are more clever than the cat and the old woman – to say nothing of myself. Don't be so conceited, child. Just thank your Maker for all the kindness we have shown you. Didn't you get into this snug room, and fall in with people who can tell you what's what? But you are such a numbskull that it's no pleasure to have you around. Believe me, I tell you this for your own good. I say unpleasant truths, but that's the only way you can know who are your friends. Be sure now that you lay some eggs. See to it that you learn to purr or to make sparks.«

»I think I'd better go out into the wide world,« said the duckling.

»Suit yourself,« said the hen.

So off went the duckling. He swam on the water, and dived down in it, but still he was slighted by every living creature because of his ugliness.

Autumn came on. The leaves in the forest turned yellow and brown. The wind took them and whirled them about. The heavens looked cold as the low clouds hung heavy with snow and hail. Perched on the fence, the raven screamed, »Caw, caw!« and trembled with cold. It made one shiver to think of it. Pity the poor little duckling!

One evening, just as the sun was setting in splendour, a great flock of large, handsome birds appeared out of the reeds. The duckling had never seen birds so beautiful. They were dazzling white, with long graceful necks. They were swans. They uttered a very strange cry as they unfurled their magnificent wings to fly from this cold land, away to warmer countries and to open waters. They went up so high, so very high, that the ugly little duckling felt a strange uneasiness come over him as he watched them. He went around and round in the water, like a wheel. He craned his neck to follow their course, and gave a cry so shrill and strange that he frightened himself. Oh! he could not forget them – those splendid, happy birds. When he could no longer see them he dived to the very bottom, and when he came up again he was quite beside himself. He did not know what birds they were or whither they were bound, yet he loved them more than anything he had ever loved before. It was not that he envied them, for how could he ever dare dream of wanting their marvelous beauty for himself? He would have been grateful if only the ducks would have tolerated him – the poor ugly creature.

The winter grew cold – so bitterly cold that the duckling had to swim to and fro in the water to keep it from freezing over. But every night the hole in which he swam kept getting smaller and smaller. Then it froze so hard that the duckling had to paddle continuously to keep the crackling ice from closing in upon him. At last, too tired to move, he was frozen fast in the ice.

Early that morning a farmer came by, and when he saw how things were he went out on the pond, broke away the ice with his wooden shoe, and carried the duckling home to his wife. There the duckling revived, but when the children wished to play with him he thought they meant to hurt him. Terrified, he fluttered into the milk pail, splashing the whole room with milk. The woman shrieked and threw up her hands as he flew into the butter tub, and then in and out of the meal barrel. Imagine what he looked like now! The woman screamed and lashed out at him with the fire tongs. The children tumbled over each other as they tried to catch him, and they laughed and they shouted. Luckily the door was open, and the duckling escaped through it into the bushes, where he lay down, in the newly fallen snow, as if in a daze.

But it would be too sad to tell of all the hardships and wretchedness he had to endure during this cruel winter. When the warm sun shone once more, the duckling was still alive among the reeds of the marsh. The larks began to sing again. It was beautiful springtime.

Then, quite suddenly, he lifted his wings. They swept through the air much more strongly than before, and their powerful strokes carried him far. Before he quite knew what was happening, he found himself in a great garden where apple trees bloomed. The lilacs filled the air with sweet scent and hung in clusters from long, green branches that bent over a winding stream. Oh, but it was lovely here in the freshness of spring!

From the thicket before him came three lovely white swans. They ruffled their feathers and swam lightly in the stream. The duckling recognized these noble creatures, and a strange feeling of sadness came upon him.

»I shall fly near these royal birds, and they will peck me to bits because I, who am so very ugly, dare to go near them. But I don't care. Better be killed by them than to be nipped by the ducks, pecked by the hens, kicked about by the henyard girl, or suffer such misery in winter.«

So he flew into the water and swam toward the splendid swans. They saw him, and swept down upon him with their rustling feathers raised. »Kill me!« said the poor creature, and he bowed his head down over the water to wait for death. But what did he see there, mirrored in the clear stream? He beheld his own image, and it was no longer the reflection of a clumsy, dirty, gray bird, ugly and offensive. He himself was a swan! Being born in a duck yard does not matter, if only you are hatched from a swan's egg.

He felt quite glad that he had come through so much trouble and misfortune, for now he had a fuller understanding of his own good fortune, and of beauty when he met with it. The great swans swam all around him and stroked him with their bills.

Several little children came into the garden to throw grain and bits of bread upon the water. The smallest child cried, »Here's a new one,« and the others rejoiced, »yes, a new one has come.« They clapped their hands, danced around, and ran to bring their father and mother.

And they threw bread and cake upon the water, while they all agreed, »The new one is the most handsome of all. He's so young and so good-looking.« The old swans bowed in his honour.

Then he felt very bashful, and tucked his head under his wing. He did not know what this was all about. He felt so very happy, but he wasn't at all proud,

for a good heart never grows proud. He thought about how he had been persecuted and scorned, and now he heard them all call him the most beautiful of all birds. The lilacs dipped their clusters into the stream before him, and the sun shone so warm and so heartening. He rustled his feathers and held his slender neck high, as he cried out with full heart, »I never dreamed there could be so much happiness, when I was the ugly duckling.«

Clumsy Hans

Out in the country there was an old mansion where an old squire lived with his two sons, who were so witty that they thought themselves too clever for words. They decided to go out and propose to the King's daughter, which they were at liberty to do, for she had announced publicly that she would take for a husband the man who had the most to say for himself.

The two brothers made their preparations eight days before. That was all the time they had, but it was enough, for they had many accomplishments, and everyone knows how useful they can be. One of them knew the whole Latin dictionary by heart and the town's newspaper for three years – so well that he could repeat it backward or forward. The other had learned all the articles of law and knew what every alderman must know; consequently, he was sure he could talk of governmental affairs, and besides this he could embroider suspenders, for he was very gentle and also clever with his fingers.

»I shall win the Princess!« they both said, as their father gave each one of them a beautiful horse. The one who had memorized the dictionary and the newspapers had a coal-black horse, while the one who knew all about

governmental affairs and could embroider had a milk-white one. Then they smeared the corners of their mouths with cod-liver oil, to make them more glib.

All the servants assembled in the courtyard to watch them mount their horses, but just then the third brother came up; for there were really three, although nobody paid much attention to the third, because he was not so learned as the other two. In fact, everybody called him »Clumsy Hans«.

»Where are you going in all your Sunday clothes?« he asked.

»To the King's court, to woo the Princess. Haven't you heard what the King's drummer is proclaiming all over the country?« Then they told him about it.

»Gracious,« said Clumsy Hans, »I guess I'll go, too!« But his brothers only burst out laughing at him as they rode away.

»Father,« shouted Clumsy Hans, »Let me have a horse. I feel like getting married, too. If she takes me, she takes me; and if she doesn't take me, I'll take her, anyway.«

»That's a lot of nonsense!« replied his father. »You'll get no horse from me. Why, you don't know how to talk properly. Now, your brothers are intelligent men.«

»If I can't have a horse I'll take the billy goat,« said Clumsy Hans. »He belongs to me, and he can carry me very well.« So he mounted the billy goat, dug his heels into its sides, and galloped off down the highway.

»Alley-oop! What a ride! Here I come!« shouted Clumsy Hans, singing so loud that his voice was heard far away.

But his two brothers rode quietly on ahead of him. They were not speaking a word to each other, for they were thinking about all the clever speeches they would have to make, and of course these had to be carefully prepared and memorized beforehand.

»Halloo!« cried Clumsy Hans. »Here I come! Look what I found on the road!« Then he showed them a dead crow he had picked up.

»Clumsy!« said the brothers. »What are you going to do with that?«

»Why, I am going to give it to the Princess!«

»Yes, you do that,« they said as they rode on laughing.

»Halloo, here I come again! Just look what I've found this time! You don't find things like this on the road every day!« So the brothers turned around to see what it was this time.

»Clumsy!« they said. »That's just an old wooden shoe, and the upper part's broken off, anyway. Is the Princess going to have that, too?«

»She certainly is,« replied Hans, and the brothers again laughed and rode on far in advance of him.

»Halloo! Here I am again,« shouted Clumsy Hans. »Now this is getting better and better! This is really something!«

»Well, what have you found this time?« asked the brothers.

»Oh, I can't really tell you,« Clumsy Hans said. »How pleased the Princess will be!«

»Uh!« said the brothers. »Why, it's nothing but mud out of the ditch!«

»Yes, of course,« said Clumsy Hans, »but the very finest sort of mud. Look, it runs right through your fingers.« Then he filled his pockets with it.

But his brothers galloped on ahead as fast as they could, and so they arrived at the town gate a full hour ahead of Hans. At the gate each suitor was given a numbered ticket, and as fast as they arrived they were arranged in rows, six to a row, packed together so tightly that they could not even move their arms. That was a wise plan, for otherwise they could have cut each other's backs to pieces, just because one stood in front of another. All the inhabitants of the town stood around the castle, peering in through the windows to watch the Princess receive her suitors; but as each young man came into the room, he became tongue-tied.

»No good!« said the Princess. »Take him away!«

Now came the brother who had memorized the dictionary, but he had completely forgotten it while standing in line. The floor creaked under his footsteps, and the ceiling was made of mirrors so that he could see himself standing on his head; and at each window stood three clerks and an alderman, writing down every word that was spoken, so that it immediately could be printed in the newspaper and sold for two pennies on the street corners.

It was a terrible ordeal, and besides there were such fires in the stoves that the pipe was red-hot.

»It's terribly hot in here,« said the suitor.

»That's because my father is roasting chickens today,« said the Princess.

»Baa!« There he stood. He was not ready for a speech of this kind and hadn't a word to say, just when he wanted to say something extremely witty. »Baa!«

»No good!« said the Princess. »Take him away!« And consequently he had to leave.

Now the second brother approached.

»It's dreadfully warm here,« he said.

»Yes, we're roasting chickens today,« replied the Princess.

»What-what did you-uh-what?« he stammered, and all the clerks carefully wrote down, »What-what did you-uh-what?«

»No good,« said the Princess again. »Out with him!«

Now it was Clumsy Hans's turn, and he rode his billy goat right into the hall.

»Terribly hot in here,« he said.

»I'm roasting young chickens,« replied the Princess.

»Why, that's fine!« said Clumsy Hans. »Then I suppose I can get my crow roasted?«

»That you can,« said the Princess. »But have you anything to roast it in? I haven't any pots or pans.«

»But I have,« replied Clumsy Hans. »Here's a cooking pot with a tin handle!« Then he pulled out the old wooden shoe and put the crow right into it.

»Why, that's enough for a whole meal!« said the Princess. »But where do we get the sauce from?«

»I have that in my pocket,« replied Clumsy Hans. »In fact, I have so much I can afford to spill some of it.« Then he poured a little of the mud from his pocket.

»I like that!« said the Princess. »You have an answer for everything, and
you know how to speak. I'll take you for my husband. But do you know that
everything we've said and are saying is written down and will be published in
the paper tomorrow? Look over there, and you'll see in each window three
clerks and an old alderman, and that alderman is the worst of all; he doesn't
understand anything!«

She said this only to frighten him, but all the clerks chuckled with delight
and spurted blots of ink on the floor.

»Oh, so these are the gentlemen!« said Clumsy Hans. »Then I must give the
alderman the best thing I have.« Then he turned out his pockets and threw
the wet mud in the face of the alderman.

»Cleverly done!« said the Princess. »I could never have done that, but I'll learn in time!«

So Clumsy Hans was made a king, with a wife and a crown, and sat on a throne. And we had this story straight from the alderman's newspaper – but that is one you can't always depend upon.

The Swineherd

Once there was a poor prince, he had a kingdom; it was very tiny. Still it was large enough to marry upon, and on marriage his heart was set.

Now it was certainly rather bold of him to say, »Will you have me?« to the Emperor's own daughter. But he did, for his name was famous, and far and near there were hundreds of Princesses who would have said, »Yes!« and »Thank you!« too. But what did the Emperor's daughter say? Well, we'll soon find out.

A rose tree grew over the grave of the Prince's father. It was such a beautiful tree. It bloomed only once in five long years, and then it bore but a single flower. Oh, that was a rose indeed! The fragrance of it would make a man forget all of his sorrows and his cares. The Prince had a nightingale too. It sang as if all the sweet songs of the world were in its little throat. The nightingale and the rose were to be gifts to the Princess. So they were sent to her in two large silver cases.

The Emperor ordered the cases carried before him, to the great hall where the Princess was playing at »visitors,« with her maids-in-waiting. They seldom did anything else. As soon as the Princess saw that the large cases contained presents, she clapped her hands in glee. »Oh,« she said, »I do hope I get a little pussy-cat.« She opened a casket and there was the splendid rose.

»Oh, how pretty it is,« said all the maids-in-waiting.

»It's more than pretty,« said the Emperor. »It's superb.«

But the Princess poked it with her finger, and she almost started to cry. »Oh fie! Papa,« she said, »it isn't artificial. It is natural.«

»Oh, fie,« said all her maids-in-waiting, »it's only natural.«

»Well,« said the Emperor, »before we fret and pout, let's see what's in the other case.« He opened it, and out came the nightingale, which sang so sweetly that for a little while no one could think of a single thing to say against it.

»*Superbe!*« – »*Charmant!*« said the maids-in-waiting with their smattering of French, each one speaking it worse than the next.

»How the bird does remind me of our lamented Empress's music box,« said one old courtier. »It has just the same tone, and the very same way of trilling.«

The Emperor wept like a child. »Ah me,« he said.

»Bird?« said the Princess. »You mean to say it's real?«

»A real live bird,« the men who had brought it assured her.

»Then let it fly and begone,« said the Princess, who refused to hear a word about the Prince, much less see him.

But it was not so easy to discourage him. He darkened his face both brown and black, pulled his hat down over his eyes, and knocked at the door.

»Hello, Emperor,« he said. »How do you do? Can you give me some work about the palace?«

»Well,« said the Emperor, »people are always looking for jobs, but let me see. I do need somebody to tend the pigs, because we've got so many of them.«

So the Prince was appointed »Imperial Pig Tender«. He was given a wretched little room down by the pigsties, and there he had to live. All day long he sat and worked, as busy as could be, and by evening he had made a neat little kettle with bells all around the brim of it. When the kettle boiled, the bells would tinkle and play the old tune:

>»*Oh, dear Augustin,*
>*All is lost, lost, lost.*«

But that was the least of it. If anyone put his finger in the steam from this kettle he could immediately smell whatever there was for dinner in any cooking-pot in town. No rose was ever like this!

Now the Princess happened to be passing by with all of her maids-in-waiting. When she heard the tune she stopped and looked pleased, for she too knew how to play »Oh, dear Augustin«. It was the only tune she did know, and she played it with one finger.

»Why, that's the very same tune I play. Isn't the swineherd highly accomplished? I say,« she ordered, »go and ask him the price of the instrument.«

So one of the maids had to go, in among the pigsties, but she put on her overshoes first.

»What will you take for the kettle?« she asked.

»I'll take ten kisses from the Princess,« said the swineherd.

Oo, for goodness' sakes!« said the maid.

»And I won't take less,« said the swineherd.

»Well, what does he say?« the Princess wanted to know.

»I can't tell you,« said the maid. »He's too horrible.«

»Then whisper it close to my ear.« She listened to what the maid had to whisper. »Oo, isn't he naughty!« said the Princess and walked right away from there. But she had not gone very far when she heard the pretty bells play again:

»*Oh, dear Augustin,*
All is lost, lost, lost.«

»I say,« the Princess ordered, »ask him if he will take his ten kisses from my maids-in-waiting.«

»No, I thank you,« said the swineherd. »Ten kisses from the Princess, or I keep my kettle.«

»Now isn't that disgusting!« said the Princess. »At least stand around me so that no one can see.«

So her maids stood around her, and spread their skirts wide, while the swineherd took his ten kisses. Then the kettle was hers.

And then the fun started. Never was a kettle kept so busy. They boiled it from morning till night. From the chamberlain's banquet to the cobbler's breakfast, they knew all that was cooked in town. The maids-in-waiting danced about and clapped their hands.

»We know who's having sweet soup and pancakes. We know who's having porridge and cutlets. Isn't it interesting?«

»Most interesting,« said the head lady of the bedchamber.

»Now, after all, I'm the Emperor's daughter,« the Princess reminded them. »Don't you tell how I got it.«

»Goodness gracious, no!« said they all.

But the swineherd – that's the Prince, for nobody knew he wasn't a real swineherd – was busy as he could be. This time he made a rattle. Swing it around, and it would play all the waltzes, jigs, and dance tunes that have been heard since the beginning of time.

»Why it's *superbe!*« said the Princess as she came by. »I never did hear better music. I say, go and ask him the price of that instrument. But mind you – no more kissing!«

»He wants a hundred kisses from the Princess,« said the maid-in-waiting who had been in to ask him.

»I believe he's out of his mind,« said the Princess, and she walked right away from there. But she had not gone very far when she said, »After all, I'm the Emperor's daughter, and it's my duty to encourage the arts. Tell him he can have ten kisses, as he did yesterday, but he must collect the rest from my maids-in-waiting.«

»Oh, but we wouldn't like that,« said the maids.

»Fiddlesticks,« said the Princess. »If he can kiss me he certainly can kiss you. Remember, I'm the one who gives you board and wages.« So the maid had to go back to the swineherd.

»A hundred kisses from the Princess,« the swineherd told her, »or let each keep his own.«

»Stand around me,« said the Princess, and all her maids-in-waiting stood in a circle to hide her while the swineherd began to collect.

»What can have drawn such a crowd near the pigsties?« the Emperor wondered, as he looked down from his balcony. He rubbed his eyes, and he put on his spectacles. »Bless my soul if those maids-in-waiting aren't up to mischief again. I'd better go see what they are up to now.«

He pulled his easy slippers up over his heels, though ordinarily he just shoved his feet in them and let them flap. Then, my! how much faster he went. As soon as he came near the pens he took very soft steps. The maids-in-waiting were so busy counting kisses, to see that everything went fair and that

he didn't get too many or too few, that they didn't notice the Emperor behind them. He stood on his tiptoes.

»Such naughtiness!« he said when he saw them kissing, and he boxed their ears with his slipper just as the swineherd was taking his eighty-sixth kiss.

»Be off with you!« the Emperor said in a rage. And both the Princess and the swineherd were turned out of his empire. And there she stood crying. The swineherd scolded, and the rain came down in torrents.

»Poor little me,« said the Princess. »If only I had married the famous Prince! Oh, how unlucky I am!«

The swineherd slipped behind a tree, wiped the brown and black off his face, threw off his ragged clothes, and showed himself in such princely garments that the Princess could not keep from curtsying.

»I have only contempt for you,« he told her. »You turned down a Prince's honest offer, and you didn't appreciate the rose or the nightingale, but you were all too ready to kiss a swineherd for a tinkling toy to amuse you. You are properly punished.«

Then the Prince went home to his kingdom, and shut and barred the door. The Princess could stay outside and sing to her heart's content:

»*Oh, dear Augustin,*
All is lost, lost, lost.«

The Tinder Box

There came a soldier marching down the high road – one, two! one, two! He had his knapsack on his back and his sword at his side as he came home from the wars. On the road he met a witch, an ugly old witch, a witch whose lower lip dangled right down on her chest.

»Good evening, soldier,« she said. »What a fine sword you've got there, and what a big knapsack. Aren't you every inch a soldier! And now you shall have money, as much as you please.«

»That's very kind, you old witch,« said the soldier.

»See that big tree.« The witch pointed to one near by them. »It's hollow to the roots. Climb to the top of the trunk and you'll find a hole through which you can let yourself down deep under the tree. I'll tie a rope around your middle, so that when you call me I can pull you up again.«

»What would I do deep down under that tree?« the soldier wanted to know.

»Fetch money,« the witch said. »Listen. When you touch the bottom you'll find yourself in a great hall. It is very bright there, because more than a hundred lamps are burning. By their light you will see three doors. Each door has a key in it, so you can open them all.

»If you walk into the first room, you'll see a large chest in the middle of the floor. On it sits a dog, and his eyes are as big as saucers. But don't worry about that. I'll give you my blue checked apron to spread out on the floor. Snatch up that dog and set him on my apron. Then you can open the chest and take out as many pieces of money as you please. They are all copper.

»But if silver suits you better, then go into the next room. There sits a dog and his eyes are as big as mill wheels. But don't you care about that. Set the dog on my apron while you line your pockets with silver.

»Maybe you'd rather have gold. You can, you know. You can have all the gold you can carry if you go into the third room. The only hitch is that there on the money-chest sits a dog, and each of his eyes is as big as the Round Tower of Copenhagen. That's the sort of dog he is. But never you mind how fierce he looks. Just set him on my apron and he'll do you no harm as you help yourself from the chest to all the gold you want.«

»That suits me,« said the soldier. »But what do you get out of all this, you old witch? I suppose that you want your share.«

»No indeed,« said the witch. »I don't want a penny of it. All I ask is for you to fetch me an old tinder box that my grandmother forgot the last time she was down there.«

»Good,« said the soldier. »Tie the rope around me.«

»Here it is,« said the witch, »and here's my blue checked apron.«

The soldier climbed up to the hole in the tree and let himself slide through it, feet foremost down into the great hall where the hundreds of lamps were burning, just as the witch had said. Now he threw open the first door he came to. Ugh! There sat a dog glaring at him with eyes as big as saucers.

»You're a nice fellow,« the soldier said, as he shifted him to the witch's apron and took all the coppers that his pockets would hold. He shut up the chest, set the dog back on it, and made for the second room. Alas and alack! There sat the dog with eyes as big as mill wheels.

»Don't you look at me like that.« The soldier set him on the witch's apron. »You're apt to strain your eyesight.« When he saw the chest brimful of silver, he threw away all his coppers and filled both his pockets and knapsack with silver alone. Then he went into the third room. Oh, what a horrible sight to see! The dog in there really did have eyes as big as the Round Tower, and when he rolled them they spun like wheels.

»Good evening,« the soldier said, and saluted, for such a dog he had never seen before. But on second glance he thought to himself, »This won't do.« So he lifted the dog down to the floor, and threw open the chest. What a sight! Here was gold and to spare. He could buy out all Copenhagen with it. He could buy all the cake-woman's sugar pigs, and all the tin soldiers, whips, and rocking horses there are in the world. Yes, *there* was really money!

In short order the soldier got rid of all the silver coins he had stuffed in his pockets and knapsack, to put gold in their place. Yes sir, he crammed all his pockets, his knapsack, his cap, and his boots so full that he could scarcely walk. Now he was made of money. Putting the dog back on the chest he banged out the door and called up through the hollow tree:

»Pull me up now, you old witch.«

»Have you got the tinder box?« asked the witch.

»Confound the tinder box,« the soldier shouted. »I clean forgot it.«

When he fetched it, the witch hauled him up. There he stood on the high road again, with his pockets, boots, knapsack and cap full of gold.

»What do you want with the tinder box?« he asked the old witch.

»None of your business,« she told him. »You've had your money, so hand over my tinder box.«

»Nonsense,« said the soldier. »I'll take out my sword and I'll cut your head off if you don't tell me at once what you want with it.«

»I won't,« the witch screamed at him.

So he cut her head off. There she lay! But he tied all his money in her apron, slung it over his shoulder, stuck the tinder box in his pocket, and struck out for town.

It was a splendid town. He took the best rooms at the best inn, and ordered all the good things he liked to eat, for he was a rich man now because he had so much money. The servant who cleaned his boots may have thought them remarkably well worn for a man of such means, but that was before he went shopping. Next morning he bought boots worthy of him, and the best clothes. Now that he had turned out to be such a fashionable gentleman, people told him all about the splendours of their town – all about their King, and what a pretty Princess he had for a daughter.

»Where can I see her?« the soldier inquired.

»You can't see her at all,« everyone said. »She lives in a great copper castle inside all sorts of walls and towers. Only the King can come in or go out of it, for it's been foretold that the Princess will marry a common soldier. The King would much rather she didn't.«

»I'd like to see her just the same,« the soldier thought. But there was no way to manage it.

Now he lived a merry life. He went to the theatre, drove about in the King's garden, and gave away money to poor people. This was to his credit, for he remembered from the old days what it feels like to go without a penny in your pocket. Now that he was wealthy and well dressed, he had all too many who called him their friend and a genuine gentleman. That pleased him.

But he spent money every day without making any, and wound up with only two coppers to his name. He had to quit his fine quarters to live in a garret, clean his own boots, and mend them himself with a darning needle. None of his friends came to see him, because there were too many stairs to climb.

One evening when he sat in the dark without even enough money to buy a candle, he suddenly remembered there was a candle end in the tinder box that he had picked up when the witch sent him down the hollow tree. He got out the tinder box, and the moment he struck sparks from the flint of it his door burst open and there stood a dog from down under the tree. It was the one with eyes as big as saucers.

»What,« said the dog, »is my lord's command?«

»What's this?« said the soldier. »Have I got the sort of tinder box that will get me whatever I want? Go get me some money,« he ordered the dog. *Zip!* The dog was gone. *Zip!* He was back again, with a bag full of copper in his mouth.

Now the soldier knew what a remarkable tinder box he had. Strike it once and there was the dog from the chest of copper coins. Strike it twice and here came the dog who had the silver. Three times brought the dog who guarded gold.

Back went the soldier to his comfortable quarters. Out strode the soldier in fashionable clothes. Immediately his friends knew him again, because they liked him so much.

Then the thought occurred to him, »Isn't it odd that no one ever gets to see the Princess? They say she's very pretty, but what's the good of it as long as she stays locked up in that large copper castle with so many towers? Why can't I see her? Where's my tinder box?« He struck a light and, *zip!* came the dog with eyes as big as saucers.

»It certainly is late,« said the soldier. »Practically midnight. But I do want a glimpse of the Princess, if only for a moment.«

Out the door went the dog, and before the soldier could believe it, here came the dog with the Princess on his back. She was sound asleep, and so pretty that anyone could see she was a Princess. The soldier couldn't keep from kissing her, because he was every inch a soldier. Then the dog took the Princess home.

Next morning when the King and Queen were drinking their tea, the Princess told them about the strange dream she'd had – all about a dog and a soldier. She'd ridden on the dog's back, and the soldier had kissed her.

»Now that was a fine story,« said the Queen. The next night one of the old ladies of the court was under orders to sit by the Princess's bed, and see whether this was a dream or something else altogether. The soldier was longing to see the pretty Princess again, so the dog came by night to take her up and away as fast as he could run. But the old lady pulled on her storm boots and ran right after them. When she saw them disappear into a large house she thought, »Now I know where it is,« and drew a big cross on the door with a piece of chalk. Then she went home to bed, and before long the dog brought the Princess home too. But when the dog saw that cross marked on the soldier's front door, he got himself a piece of chalk and cross-marked every door in the town. This was a clever thing to do, because now the old lady couldn't tell the right door from all the wrong doors he had marked.

Early in the morning along came the King and Queen, the old lady, and all the officers, to see where the Princess had been.

»Here it is,« said the King when he saw the first cross mark.

»No, my dear. There it is,« said the Queen who was looking next door.

»Here's one, there's one, and yonder's another one!« said they all. Wherever they looked they saw chalk marks, so they gave up searching.

The Queen, though, was an uncommonly clever woman, who could do more than ride in a coach. She took her big gold scissors, cut out a piece of silk, and made a neat little bag. She filled it with fine buckwheat flour and tied it on to the Princess's back. Then she pricked a little hole in it so that the flour would sift out along the way, wherever the Princess might go.

Again the dog came in the night, took the Princess on his back, and ran with her to the soldier, who loved her so much that he would have been glad to be a Prince just so he could make her his wife.

The dog didn't notice how the flour made a trail from the castle right up to the soldier's window, where he ran up the wall with the Princess. So in the morning it was all too plain to the King and Queen just where their daughter had been.

They took the soldier and they put him in prison. There he sat. It was dark, and it was dismal, and they told him, »Tomorrow is the day for you to hang.« That didn't cheer him up any, and as for his tinder box he'd left it behind at the inn. In the morning he could see through his narrow little window how the people all hurried out of town to see him hanged. He heard the drums beat and he saw the soldiers march. In the crowd of running people he saw a shoemaker's boy in a leather apron and slippers. The boy galloped so fast that off flew one slipper, which hit the wall right where the soldier pressed his face to the iron bars.

»Hey there, you shoemaker's boy, there's no hurry,« the soldier shouted. »Nothing can happen till I get there. But if you run to where I live and bring me my tinder box, I'll give you four coppers. Put your best foot foremost.«

The shoemaker's boy could use four coppers, so he rushed the tinder box to the soldier, and – well, now we shall hear what happened!

Outside the town a high gallows had been built. Around it stood soldiers and many hundred thousand people. The King and Queen sat on a splendid throne, opposite the judge and the whole council. The soldier already stood upon the ladder, but just as they were about to put the rope around his neck he said the custom was to grant a poor criminal one last small favour. He wanted to smoke a pipe of tobacco – the last he'd be smoking in this world.

The King couldn't refuse him, so the soldier struck fire from his tinder box, once – twice – and a third time. *Zip!* There stood all the dogs, one with eyes as big as saucers, one with eyes as big as mill wheels, one with eyes as big as the Round Tower of Copenhagen.

»Help me. Save me from hanging!« said the soldier. Those dogs took the judges and all the council, some by the leg and some by the nose, and tossed them so high that they came down broken to bits.

»Don't!« cried the King, but the biggest dog took him and the Queen too, and tossed them up after the others. Then the soldiers trembled and the people shouted, »Soldier, be our King and marry the pretty Princess.«

So they put the soldier in the King's carriage. All three of his dogs danced in front of it, and shouted »Hurrah!« The boys whistled through their fingers, and the soldiers saluted. The Princess came out of the copper castle to be Queen, and that suited her exactly. The wedding lasted all of a week, and the three dogs sat at the table, with their eyes opened wider than ever before.

The Elf Mound

Several lizards darted briskly in and out of the cracks of a hollow tree. They understood each other perfectly, for they all spoke lizard language.

»My! How it rumbles and buzzes in the old elf mound,« said one lizard. »It rumbles and bumbles so that I haven't had a wink of sleep for the past two nights. I might as well have a toothache, for that also prevents me from sleeping.«

»There's something afoot,« said another lizard. »Until the cock crowed for dawn, they had the mound propped up on four red poles to give it a thoroughgoing airing. And the elf maidens are learning to stamp out some new dances. Something is surely afoot.«

»Yes, I was just talking about it with an earthworm I know,« said a third lizard, »He came straight from the mound, where he has been nosing around night and day. He overheard a good deal. For he can't see, poor thing, but he knows his way around and makes an uncommonly good eavesdropper. They expect company in the elf mound, distinguished visitors, but the earthworm wouldn't say who they are. Or maybe he didn't know. All the will-o'-the-wisps have been told to parade with their torches, as they are called, and all of the flat silver and gold plate with which the mound is well stocked is being polished and put out in the moonlight.«

»Who can the visitors be?« the lizards all wanted to know. »What in the world is going on? Listen to the hustle! Listen to the bustle!«

Just at that moment the elf mound opened, and an oldmaid elf minced out of it. The woman had no back, but otherwise she was quite properly dressed, with her amber jewelry in the shape of a heart. She kept house for her distant cousin, the old king of the elves, and she was very spry in the legs. Trip, trot,

away she went. How she hurried and scurried off to see the night raven down in the marsh.

»You are hereby invited to the elf mound, this very night,« she told him. »But may I ask you to do us a great favour first? Please deliver the other invitations for us. As you have no place of your own where you can entertain, you must make yourself generally useful. We shall have some very distinguished visitors – goblins of rank, let me tell you. So the old elf king wants to make the best impression he can.«

»Who is being invited?« the night raven asked.

»Oh, everybody may come to the big ball – even ordinary mortals if they talk in their sleep or can do anything else that we can do. But at the banquet the company must be strictly select. Only the very best people are invited to it. I've threshed that out thoroughly with the elf king, because I insist we should not even invite ghosts. First of all, we must invite the old man of the sea and his daughters. I suppose they won't like to venture out on dry land, but we can at least give them a comfortable wet stone to sit on, or something better, and I don't think they'll refuse this time. Then we must have all the old trolls of the first degree, with tails. We must ask the old man of the stream, and the pixies, and I believe we should ask the grave-pig, the bone-horse, and the church dwarf, though they live under churches and, properly speaking, belong to the clergy, who are not our sort of people at all. Still that is their vocation, and they are closely related to us, and often come to call.«

»Cra!« said the night raven as he flew to summon the guests.

On their mound, the elf maidens had already begun to dance, and they danced with long scarves made of mist and moonlight. To those who care for scarf dancing, it was most attractive.

The large central hall of the elf mound had been especially prepared for this great night. The floor was washed with moonlight, and the walls were polished with witch wax, which made them glisten like the petals of a tulip. The kitchen abounded with skewered frogs, snake skins stuffed with small children's fingers, fungus salad made of mushroom-seed, wet mouse noses, and hemlock. There was beer of the swamp witch's brewing, and sparkling saltpetre champagne from graveyard vaults. All very substantial! Rusty nails and ground glass from church windows were among the delicacies.

The old elf king had his gold crown polished with powdered slate pencil. It was a prize pupil's slate pencil, and a prize pupil's slate pencil is not so easy

for an elf king to obtain. The curtains in the bedroom were freshly starched with snail slime. Oh, how they did hustle and bustle.

»Now we shall burn horsehair and pig's bristles for incense, and my duty is done,« said the housekeeper.

»Dear papa elf,« said his youngest daughter, »will you tell me now who the guests of honour are to be?«

»Well,« he said, »it's high time that I told you. I have made a match for two of my daughters. Two of you must be ready to get married without fail. The venerable goblin chief of Norway, who lives in the old Dovrefield Mountains, and possesses a gold mine and crag castles and strongholds much better than people can imagine, is on his way here with his two sons, and each son wants a wife. The old goblin chief is a real Norwegian, honest and true, straightforward and merry. I have known him for many a year, and we drank to our lasting friendship when he came here to get his wife. She's dead now, but she was the daughter of the king of the chalk cliffs at Möen. I used to tell him that he got married on the chalk, as if he had bought his wife on credit. How I look forward to seeing him again. His sons, they say, are rough and rowdy, which, however, may not be a fair judgement. But they'll improve when they get older. It's up to you to polish them.«

»How soon will they come?« one of his daughters asked.

»That depends on the wind and the weather,« he said. »They are thrifty travellers, they will come by ship when they have a chance. I wanted them to travel overland, by way of Sweden, but the old gentleman wouldn't hear of it. He doesn't keep up with the times, and I don't like that.«

Just then two will-o'-the-wisps came tumbling in, one faster than the other and therefore he got there first. Both of them were shouting:

»Here they come, here they come!«

»Hand me my crown. Let me stand where the moon shines most brightly,« the elf king said.

His daughters lifted their long scarves and curtsied low to the ground.

There came the venerable goblin chief from the Dovrefjeld, crowned with

110

sparkling icicles and polished fir cones, muffled in his bearskin coat, and wearing his sledge-boots. His sons dressed quite differently, with their throats uncovered and without suspenders. They were husky fellows.

»Is that a hill?« The smallest of the two brothers pointed his finger at the elf mound. »In Norway we would call it a hole.«

»Son!« cried the old goblin chief. »Hills come up, and holes go down. Have you no eyes in your head?«

The only thing that amazed them, they said, was the language that people spoke here. Why, they could actually understand it.

»Don't make such tomfools of yourselves,« said their father, »or people will think you are ignoramuses.«

They entered the elf mound, where all the best people were gathered,

though they had assembled so fast that they seemed swept in by the wind. Nevertheless the arrangements were delightfully convenient for everybody. The old man of the sea and his daughters were seated at the table in large casks of water, which they said made them feel right at home. Everyone had good table manners except the two young Norwegian goblins, who put their feet on the table as if anything they did were all right.

»Take your feet out of your plates,« said the old goblin chief, and they obeyed, but not right away. They had brought fir cones in their pockets to tickle the ladies sitting next to them. To make themselves comfortable they pulled off their boots and gave them to the ladies to hold. However, their father, the old Dovre goblin, conducted himself quite differently. He talked well of the proud crags of Norway, and of waterfalls rushing down in a cloud of spray, with a roar like thunder and the sound of an organ. He told how the salmon leapt up through the waterfall, when they hear the nixes twang away on golden harps. He described bracing winter nights on which the sleigh bells chime, and boys with flaming torches skim over polished ice so clear that one can see the startled fish swish away underfoot. Yes, he had a way of talking that made you both hear and see the sawmill working and the boys and girls as they sang and danced the Norwegian Hallinge dance. Hurrah! In the wink of an eye the goblin chief gave the old-maid elf such a kiss that it smacked, though they were not in the least related.

Then the elf maidens were to do their dances, first the ordinary dances and then the dance where they stamped their feet, which set them off to perfection. Then they did a really complicated one called, »A dance to end dancing.« Keep us and save us, how light they were on their feet. Whose leg was whose? Which were arms and which were legs? They whipped through the air like shavings at a planing mill. The girls twirled so fast that it made the bone-horse's head spin, and he staggered away from the table.

»Whir-r-r,« said the goblin chief. »The girls are lively enough, but what can they do besides dancing like mad, spinning like tops, and making the bone-horse dizzy?«

»I'll show you what they can do,« the elf king boasted. He called his youngest daughter. She was as thin and fair as moonlight. She was the daintiest of all the sisters, and when she took a white wand in her mouth it vanished away. That was what she could do. But the goblin chief said this was an art he would not like his wife to possess, and he did not think his sons would either.

The second daughter could walk alongside herself as if she had a shadow, which is something that trolls do not possess. The third was a very different sort of girl. She had studied brewing with the swamp witch, and she was a good hand at seasoning alder stumps with glow worms.

»Now this one would make a good housewife,« said the goblin chief, winking instead of drinking to her, for he wanted to keep his wits clear.

The fourth daughter played upon a tall, golden harp. As soon as she fingered the first string everyone kicked up his left leg, for all of the troll tribe are left-legged. And as soon as she fingered the second string, everyone had to do just as she said.

»What a dangerous woman,« said the goblin chief. His sons were very bored, and they strolled out of the elf mound as their father asked, »What can the next daughter do?«

»I have learned to like Norwegians,« she told him. »I'll never marry unless I can live in Norway.«

But her youngest sister whispered in the old goblin's ear, »She only says that because of the old Norwegian saying, that even though the world should fall the rocks of Norway would still stand tall, that's why she wants to go there. She's afraid to die.«

»Hee, hee,« said the goblin, »somebody let the cat out of the bag. Now for the seventh and last.«

»The sixth comes before the seventh,« said the elf king, who was more careful with his arithmetic. But his sixth daughter would not come forward.

»I can only tell the truth,« she said, »so nobody likes me, and I have enough to do to sew upon my shroud.«

Now came the seventh and last daughter. What could she do? She could tell tales, as many as ever she pleased.

»Here are my five fingers,« said the old goblin. »Tell me a story for each of them.«

The elf maiden took him by the wrist, and he chuckled till he almost choked. When she came to the fourth finger, which wore a gold ring just as if it knew that weddings were in the air, the old goblin said, »Hold it fast, for I give you my hand. I'll take you as my wife.«

The elf maiden said that the stories of Culdbrand, the fourth finger, and of little Peter Playfellow, the fifth finger, remained to be told.

»Ah, we shall save those until winter,« said the old goblin chief. »Then you shall tell me about the fir tree and the birch; of the ghost presents and of the creaking frost. You will be our teller of tales, for none of us has the knack of it. We shall sit in my great stone castle where the pine logs blaze, and we shall drink our mead out of the golden horns of old Norwegian kings. I have two that the water goblin washed into my hand. And while we sit there side by side, Sir Carbo will come to call, and he will sing you the mountain maidens' song. How merry we then shall be! The salmon will leap in the waterfall, and beat against our stone walls, but he'll never get in to where we sit so snug. Ah, I tell you, it is good to live in glorious old Norway. But where have the boys gone?«

Where indeed? They were charging through the fields, blowing out the will-o'-the-wisps who were coming so modestly for their torchlight parade.

»Is that a way to behave?« said the goblin chief. »I have chosen a step-mother for you, so come and choose wives of your own.«

But his sons said they preferred speeches and drink to matrimony. So they made speeches, and they drank health, and turned their glasses bottom upside down to show how empty they were. Then they took off their coats, and lay down on the table to sleep, for they had no manners. But the old goblin danced around the room with his young bride, and changed his boots for hers, which was much more fashionable than merely exchanging rings.

»There's that cock crowing!« the old-maid housekeeper of the elves warned them. »Now we must close the shutters to keep the sun from burning us.«

So they closed the mound. But outside the lizards darted around the hollow tree, and one said to the other: »Oh, how we liked that old Norwegian goblin chief!«

»I preferred his jolly sons,« said the earthworm, but then he had no eyes in his head, poor thing.

The Shepherdess
and the Chimney-Sweep

Have you ever seen a very old chest, black with age, and covered with outlandish carved ornaments and curling leaves? Well, in a certain parlour there was just such a chest, handed down from some great-grandmother. Carved all up and down it ran tulips and roses – odd-looking flourishes – and from fanciful thickets little stags stuck out their antlered heads.

Right in the middle of the chest a whole man was carved. He made you laugh to look at him grinning away, though one could not call his grinning laughing. He had hind legs like a goat's, little horns on his forehead, and a long beard. All the children called him »General Headquarters-Hindquarters-Gives-Orders-Front-and-Rear-Sergeant-Billygoat-Legs.« It was a difficult name to pronounce and not many people get to be called by it, but he must have been very important or why should anyone have taken the trouble to carve him at all?

However, there he stood, forever eyeing a delightful little china shepherdess on the table top under the mirror. The little shepherdess wore golden shoes, and looped up her gown fetchingly with a red rose. Her hat was gold, and even her crook was gold. She was simply charming!

Close by her stood a little chimney-sweep, as black as coal, but made of porcelain too. He was as clean and tidy as anyone can be, because you see he was only an ornamental chimney-sweep. If the china-makers had wanted to, they could just as easily have turned him out as a prince, for he had a jaunty way of holding his ladder, and his cheeks were as pink as a girl's. That was a

116

mistake, don't you think? He should have been dabbed with a pinch or two of soot.

He and the shepherdess stood quite close together. They had both been put on the table where they stood and, having been placed there, they had become engaged because they suited each other exactly. Both were young, both were made of the same porcelain, so they were equally fragile.

Near them stood another figure, three times as big as they were. It was an old Chinaman who could nod his head. He too was made of porcelain, and he said he was the little shepherdess's grandfather. But he could not prove it. Nevertheless he claimed that this gave him authority over her, and when General-Headquarters-Hindquarters-Gives-Orders-Front-and-Rear-Sergeant-Billygoat-Legs asked for her hand in marriage, the old Chinaman had nodded consent.

»There's a husband for you!« the old Chinaman told the shepherdess. »A husband who, I am inclined to believe, is made of mahogany. He can make you Mrs. General-Headquarters-Hindquarters-Gives-Orders-Front-and-Rear-Sergeant-Billygoat-Legs. He has the whole chest full of silver, and who knows what else he's got hidden away in his secret drawers?«

»But I don't want to go and live in the dark chest,« said the little shepherdess. »I have heard people say he's got eleven china wives in there already.«

»Then you will make twelve,« said the Chinaman. »Tonight, as soon as the old chest commences to creak I'll marry you off to him, as sure as I'm a Chinaman.« Then he nodded off to sleep. The little shepherdess cried and looked at her true love, the porcelain chimney-sweep.

»Please let's run away into the big, wide world,« she begged him, »for we can't stay here.«

»I'll do just what you want me to,« the little chimneysweep told her. »Let's run away right now. I feel sure I can support you by chimney-sweeping.«

»I wish we were safely down off this table,« she said. »I'll never be happy until we are out in the big, wide world.«

117

He told her not to worry, and showed her how to drop her little feet over the table edge, and bow to step from one gilded leaf to another down the carved leg of the table. He set up his ladder to help her, and down they came safely to the floor. But when they glanced at the old chest they saw a great commotion. All the carved stags were craning their necks, tossing their antlers, and turning their heads. General-Headquarters-Hindquarters-Gives-Orders-Front-and-Rear-Sergeant-Billygoat-Legs jumped high in the air, and shouted to the old Chinaman, »They're running away! They're running away!«

This frightened them so that they jumped quickly into a drawer of the window-seat. Here they found three or four decks of cards, not quite complete, and a little puppet theatre, which was set up as well as it was possible to do. A play was in progress, and all the diamond queens, heart queens, club queens, and spade queens sat in the front row and fanned themselves with the tulips they held in their hands. Behind them the knaves lined up, showing that they had heads both at the top and at the bottom, as face cards do have. The play was all about two people who were not allowed to marry, and it made the shepherdess cry because it was so like her own story.

»I can't bear to see any more,« she said. »I must get out of this drawer at once.« But when they got back to the floor and looked up at the table, they saw that the old Chinaman was wide awake now. Not only his head, but his whole body rocked forward. The lower part of his body was one solid piece, you see.

»The old Chinaman's coming!« cried the little Shepherdess, who was so upset that she fell down on her porcelain knees.

»I have an idea,« said the chimney-sweep. »We'll hide in the pot-pourri vase in the corner. There we can rest upon rose petals and lavender, and when he finds us we can throw salt in his eyes.«

»It's no use,« she said. »Besides, I know the pot-pourri vase was once the old Chinaman's sweetheart, and where there used to be love a little affection is sure to remain. No, there's nothing for us to do but to run away into the big wide world.«

»Are you really so brave that you'd go into the wide world with me?« asked the chimney-sweep. »Have you thought about how big it is, and that we can never come back here?«

»I have,« she said.

The chimney-sweep looked her straight in the face and said, »My way lies up through the chimney. Are you really so brave that you'll come with me into the stove, and crawl through the stovepipe? It will take us to the chimney. Once we get there, I'll know what to do. We shall climb so high that they'll never catch us, and at the very top there's an opening into the big wide world.«

He led her to the stove door.

»It looks very black in there,« she said. But she let him lead her through the stove and through the stovepipe, where it was pitch-black night.

»Now we've come to the chimney,« he said. »And see! See how the bright star shines over our heads.«

A real star, high up in the heavens, shone down as if it wished to show them the way. They clambered and scuffled, for it was hard climbing and terribly steep-way, way up high! But he lifted her up, and held her safe, and found the best places for her little porcelain feet. At last they reached the top of the chimney, where they sat down. For they were so tired, and no wonder!

Overhead was the starry sky, and spread before them were all the housetops in the town. They looked out on the big wide world. The poor shepherdess had never thought it would be like that. She flung her little head against the chimneysweep, and sobbed so many tears that the gilt washed off her sash.

»This is too much,« she said. »I can't bear it. The wide world is too big. Oh! If I only were back on my table under the mirror. I'll never be happy until I stand there again, just as before. I followed you faithfully out into the world, and if you love me the least bit you'll take me right home.«

The chimney-sweep tried to persuade her that it was not sensible to go back. He talked to her about the old Chinaman, and of General-Head-quarters-Hindquarters-Gives-Orders-Front-and-Rear-Sergeant-Billygoat-Legs, but she sobbed so hard and kissed her chimney-sweep so much that he had to do as she said, though he thought it was the wrong thing to do.

So back down the chimney they climbed with great difficulty, and they crawled through the wretched stovepipe into the dark stove. Here they

listened behind the door, to find out what was happening in the room. Everything seemed quiet, so they opened the door and-oh, what a pity! There on the floor lay the Chinaman, in three pieces. When he had come running after them, he tumbled off the table and smashed. His whole back had come off in one piece, and his head had rolled into the corner. General-Head-quarters-Hindquarters-Gives-Orders-Front-and-Rear-Sergeant-Billygoat-Legs was standing where he always stood, looking thoughtful.

»Oh, dear,« said the little shepherdess, »poor old grand father is all broken up, and it's entirely our fault. I shall never live through it.« She wrung her delicate hands.

»He can be patched,« said the chimney-sweep. »He can be riveted. Don't be so upset about him. A little glue for his back and a strong rivet in his neck, and he will be just as good as new, and just as disagreeable as he was before.«

»Will he, really?« she asked, as they climbed back to their old place on the table.

»Here we are,« said the chimney-sweep. »Back where we started from. We could have saved ourselves a lot of trouble.«

»Now if only old grandfather were mended,« said the little shepherdess. »Is mending terribly expensive?«

He was mended well enough. The family had his back glued together, and a strong rivet put through his neck. That made him as good as new, except that never again could he nod his head.

»It seems to me that you have grown haughty since your fall, though I don't see why you should be proud of it,« General-Headquarters-Hindquarters-Gives-Orders-Front-and-Rear-Sergeant-Billygoat-Legs complained. »Am I to have her, or am I not?«

The chimney-sweep and the little shepherdess looked so pleadingly at the old Chinaman, for they were deathly afraid he would nod. But he did not. He could not. And neither did he care to tell anyone that, forever and a day, he would have to wear a rivet in his neck.

So the little porcelain people remained together. They thanked goodness for the rivet in grandfather's neck, and they kept on loving each other until the day they broke.

What the Old Man Does Is Always Right

Now I am going to tell you a story that I heard when I was a little fellow and that I like better and better the more I think of it. For it's the same with stories as with many people; the older they grow, the nicer they grow, and that is delightful.

You have been out in the country, of course. There you must have seen a really old farmhouse with a thatched roof, where moss and weeds have planted themselves; a stork's nest decorates the chimney (you can never do without the stork); the walls are slanting; the windows are low (in fact, only one of them was made to open); the baking oven sticks out like a fat little stomach; and an elderbush leans over the gate, where you can see a tiny pond with a duck or ducklings, under a gnarled willow tree. Yes, and then, of course, there's a watchdog which barks at everybody and everything.

Well, there was a farmhouse just like that out in the country, and in it lived two people, a farmer and his wife. They had few enough possessions, but still there was one they could do without, and that was a horse, which grazed along the ditch beside the highway. The old farmer used it to ride to town and lent it to his neighbours, receiving some slight services from them in return, but still it would be much more profitable to sell the horse, or at least exchange it for something that would be more useful to them.

But which should they do, sell or trade?

»You'll know what's best, Father,« said the wife. »It's market day. Come on,

124

ride off to town, and get money for the horse, or make a good bargain with it. Whatever you do is always right; so be off for the market!«

So she tied on his neckerchief – for that was something she understood much better than he – tied it with a double bow, and made him look quite dashing. She brushed his hat with the palm of her hand, and she kissed him on his mouth, and then off he went, riding the horse that was to be either sold or bartered. Of course, he would know the right thing to do.

The sun was scorching, and there was not a cloud in the sky. The road was dusty, and crowded with people on their way to market, some in wagons, some on horseback, and some on their own two legs. Yes, it was a fierce sun, with no shade all the way.

Now a man came along, driving a cow, as pretty a cow as you could wish to see. »I'm sure she must give grand milk,« thought the peasant. »It would be a pretty good bargain if I got her. Hey, you with the cow!« he said. »Let's have a little talk. Look here, I believe a horse costs more than a cow, but it doesn't matter to me, since I have more use for a cow. Shall we make a swap?«

»Fair enough,« said the man with the cow; and so they swapped.

Now the farmer might just as well have turned home again, for he had finished his business. But he had planned to go to market, so to market he would go, if only to watch; hence, with his cow, he continued on his way. He walked fast, and so did the cow, and pretty soon they overtook a man who was leading a sheep; it was a fine-looking sheep, in good condition and well clothed with wool.

»I certainly would like to have that,« thought the peasant. »It would find plenty of grazing beside our ditch, and in the winter we could keep it in our own room. It would really be much more sensible for us to be keeping a sheep rather than a cow. Shall we trade?«

Yes, the sheep's owner was quite willing, so the exchange was made, and now the farmer went on along the highway with his sheep. Near a stile he met a man with a big goose under his arm.

»Well, you've got a fine heavy fellow there!« said the farmer. »It's got plenty of feathers and fat! How nice it would be to have it tied up near our little pond, and, besides, it would be something for Mother to save the scraps for. She has often said, 'If we only had a goose.' Now she can have one – and she shall, too! Will you swap? I'll give you my sheep for your goose, and my thanks, too.«

The other had no objection, so they swapped, and the farmer got the goose. By now he was close to the town; the road was getting more and more crowded, people and cattle pushing past him, thronging in the road, in the ditch, and right up to the tollkeeper's potato patch, where his one hen was tied up, in case it should lose its head in a panic and get lost. It was a bobtailed hen that winked with one eye and looked in good condition.

»Cluck, cluck,« it said; what it meant by that, I would not know; but what the peasant thought when he saw it was this, »She's the prettiest hen I've ever seen – much prettier than any of our parson's brood hens. I would certainly like to have her. A hen can always find a grain of corn, and she can almost provide for herself. I almost think it would be a good idea to take her instead of the goose. Shall we trade?« he asked.

»Trade?« said the other. »Well, not a bad idea.« And so they traded. The tollkeeper got the goose, and the farmer got the hen.

He had completed a good deal of business since he started for town; it was hot, and he was tired. What he needed was a drink and a bite to eat.

He had reached an inn and was ready to enter, when the innkeeper's helper met him in the doorway, carrying a sackful of something.

»What have you got there?« asked the farmer.

»Rotten apples,« was the answer. »A whole sackful for the pigs.«

»What a lot! Wouldn't Mother like to see so many! Why, last year we had only one single apple on the old tree by the peat shed. That apple was to be kept, and it stood on the chest of drawers till it burst. 'That is always a sign of prosperity,' Mother said. Here she could see plenty of prosperity! Yes, I only wish she could have it!«

»Well, what'll you give me for them?« asked the innkeeper's helper.

»Give for them? Why, I'll give you my hen!« So he turned over the hen, took the apples, and went into the inn, straight up to the bar; he set his sack upright against the stove, without noticing that there was a fire in it. There were a number of strangers present, horse dealers, cattle dealers, and two Englishmen so rich that their pockets were bursting with gold coins. They were fond of making bets, as Englishmen in stories always are.

»Suss! Suss! Suss!« What was that noise at the stove? It was the apples beginning to roast!

»What's that?« everybody said, and they soon found out. They were hearing the whole story of the horse that had been traded first for a cow and finally for a sack of rotten apples.

»Well, you'll get a good beating from your old woman when you go home!« said the Englishmen. »You're in for a rough time.«

»I'll get kisses, not cuffs,« said the farmer. »Mother will say, 'Whatever the old man does is right'.«

»Shall we bet on it?« said the Englishmen. »We have gold by the barrel! A hundred pounds sterling to a hundred-pound weight?«

»Let's say a bushelful,« replied the peasant. »I can only bet my bushel of apples, and throw in myself and the old woman, but I think that'll be more than full measure.«

»That's a bet!« the Englishmen cried, and the bet was made! So the innkeeper's cart was brought out, the Englishmen got into it, the farmer got into it, the rotten apples got into it, and away they went to the old man's cottage.

»Good evening, Mother.«

»Same to you, Father.«

»Well, I've made the bargain.«

»Yes, you know how to do business,« said the wife, and gave him a big hug, forgetting both the sack and the strangers.

»I traded the horse for a cow.«

»Thank God for the milk!« said the wife. »Now we can have milk, butter, and cheese on our table! What a splendid swap!«

»Yes, but I swapped the cow for a sheep.«

»That's still better!« cried the wife. »You're always so thoughtful. We have plenty of grass for a sheep. But now we'll have sheep's milk, and sheep's cheese, and woolen stockings, yes, and a woolen nightgown, too. A cow couldn't give us that; she loses all her hairs. But you're always such a thoughtful husband.«

»But then I exchanged the sheep for a goose.«

»What! Will we really have goose for Michaelmas this year, dear Father? You always think of what would please me, and that was a beautiful thought! We can tie up the goose, and it'll grow even fatter for Michaelmas Day.«

»But I traded the goose for a hen,« continued the peasant.

»A hen? Well, that was a fine trade!« replied his wife. »A hen will lay eggs and sit on them and we'll have chickens. Imagine, a chicken yard! Just the thing I've always wanted most!«

»Yes, but I exchanged the hen for a sack of rotten apples.«

»Then I must certainly give you a kiss!« said the wife. »Thank you, my own

husband. And now I have something to tell you. When you had gone I decided I'd get a fine dinner ready for you – omelet with chives. Now I had the eggs all right, but no chives. So I went over to the schoolmaster's, because I know they have chives; but that sweet woman is so stingy she wanted something in return. What could I give her? Nothing grows in our garden, not even a rotten apple; I didn't even have that for her. But now I can give her ten or even a whole sackful! Isn't it funny, Father!« she said, and kissed him right on his mouth.

»I like that!« cried both the Englishmen. »Always downhill, but always happy. That alone is worth the money!« So they were quite content to pay the bushelful of gold pieces to the peasant, who had got kisses instead of cuffs for his bargains.

Yes, it always pays when the wife believes and admits that her husband is the wisest man in the world and that whatever he does is right.

Well, this is the story. I heard it when I was a youngster, an now you've heard it, too, so you know that what the old man does is always right.

The Little Match Girl

It was so terribly cold. Snow was falling, and it was almost dark. Evening came on, the last evening of the year. In the cold and gloom a poor little girl, bareheaded and barefoot, was walking through the streets. Of course when she had left her house she had been wearing slippers, but what good had they been? They were very big slippers, way too big for her, for they belonged to her mother. The little girl had lost them running across the road, where two carriages had rattled by terribly fast. One slipper she had not been able to find again, and a boy had run off with the other, saying he could use it very well as a cradle some day when he had children of his own. And so the little girl walked on her naked feet, which were quite red and blue with the cold. In an old apron she carried several packages of matches, and she held a box of them in her hand. No one had bought any from her all day long, and no one had given her a penny.

Shivering with cold and hunger, she crept along, a picture of misery, poor little girl! The snowflakes fell on her long fair hair, which hung in pretty curls over her neck. But she did not think of her pretty curls now. In all the windows lights were shining, and there was a wonderful smell of roast goose, for it was New Year's Eve. Yes, she thought of that!

In a corner formed by two houses, one of which projected farther out into the street than the other, she sat down and drew up her little feet under her. She was getting colder and colder, but did not dare to go home, for she had sold no matches, nor earned a single penny, and her father would surely beat her. Besides, it was cold at home, for they had nothing over them but a roof through which the wind whistled even though the biggest cracks had been stuffed with straw and rags.

Her hands were almost dead with cold. Oh, how much one little match might warm her! If she could only take one from the box and rub it against the wall and warm her hands. She drew one out. R-r-ratch! How it sputtered and burned! It made a warm, bright flame, like a little candle, as she held her hands over it; but it gave a strange light! It really seemed to the little girl as if she were sitting before a great iron stove with shiny brass knobs and a brass cover. How wonderfully the fire burned! How comfortable it was! The youngster stretched out her feet to warm them too; then the little flame went out, the stove vanished, and she had only the remains of the burnt match in her hand.

She struck another match against the wall. It burned brightly, and when the light fell upon the wall it became transparent like a thin veil, and she could see through it into a room. On the table a snow-white cloth was spread, and on it stood the finest china. The roast goose steamed gloriously, stuffed with apples and prunes. And what was still better, the goose jumped down from the dish and waddled along the floor, with a knife and fork in its breast, right over to the little girl. Then the match went out, and she could see only the thick, cold wall. She lighted another match. Then she was sitting under the most beautiful Christmas tree. It was much larger and much more beautiful than the one she had seen last Christmas through the glass door at the rich merchant's home. Thousands of candles burned on the green branches, and coloured pictures like those in the printshops looked down at her. The little girl reached both her hands toward them. Then the match went out. But the Christmas lights mounted higher. She saw them now as bright stars in the sky. One of them fell down, forming a long line of fire.

»Now someone is dying,« thought the little girl, for her old grandmother, the only person who had loved her, and who was now dead, had told her that when a star fell down a soul went up to God.

She rubbed another match against the wall. It became bright again, and in the glow the old grandmother stood clear and shining, kind and lovely.

»Grandmother!« cried the child. »Oh, take me with you! I know you will

132

disappear when the match burns out. You will vanish like the warm stove, the wonderful roast goose and the beautiful big Christmas tree!«

And she quickly struck the whole bundle of matches, for she wished to keep her grandmother with her. And the matches burned with such a glow that it became brighter than daylight. Grandmother had never been so grand and beautiful. She took the little girl in her arms, and both of them flew in brightness and joy above the earth, very, very high, and up there was neither cold, nor hunger, nor fear – they were with God.

But in the corner, leaning against the wall, sat the little girl with red cheeks and a smile on her face, frozen to death on the last evening of the old year. The

New Year's sun rose upon the little dead body. The child sat there, stiff and cold, holding the matches, of which one bundle was almost burned.

»She wanted to warm herself,« the people said. No one imagined what beautiful things she had seen, and how happily she had gone with her old grandmother into the bright New Year.

It's Quite True!

»It's a dreadful story!« said a hen, and she said it in a part of town, too, where it had not taken place. »It's a dreadful story to happen in a henhouse. I'm afraid to sleep alone tonight; it's a good thing, there are many of us on the perch!« And then she told a story that made the feathers of the other hens stand on end and the rooster's comb fall. It's quite true!

But we will begin at the beginning and tell what had happened in a henhouse at the other end of town.

The sun went down, and the hens flew up. One of them was a white-feathered and short-limbed hen who laid her eggs according to the regulations and who was a respectable hen in every way. As she settled herself on the perch, she plucked herself with her beak, and a tiny feather came out.

»There it goes,« she said. »No doubt the more I pluck, the more beautiful I will get.« But she said it only in fun, for she was considered the jolliest among the hens, although, as we've said before, most respectable. Then she fell asleep.

There was darkness all around, and the hens sat closely together. But the hen that sat closest to the white hen was not asleep; she had heard and had not heard, as one should do in this world, if one wishes to live in peace. But still she could not resist telling it to her nearest neighbour.

»Did you hear what was said? Well, I don't want to mention any names, but there is a hen here who intends to pluck out all her feathers just to make herself look well. If I were a rooster, I would despise her.«

Right above the hens lived a mother owl with a father owl and all her little owls. They had sharp ears in that family, and they all heard every word that their neighbour hen had said. They all rolled their eyes, and the mother owl flapped her wings and said; »Don't listen to it. But I suppose you all heard what was said. I heard it with my own ears, and one must hear a great deal before they fall off. One of the hens has so completely forgotten what is becoming conduct to a hen that she plucks out all her feathers, while the rooster watches her.«

»Little pitchers have big ears,« said the father owl. »Children shouldn't hear such talk.«

»I must tell it to the owl across the road,« said the mother owl. »She is such a respectable owl!« And away flew Mamma.

»Hoo-whoo! Hoo-whoo!« they both hooted to the pigeons in the pigeon house across the road. »Have you heard it? Have you heard it? Hoo-whoo! There is a hen who has plucked out all her feathers just to please the rooster.

She must be freezing to death; that is, if she isn't dead already. Hoo-whoo! Hoo-whoo!«

»Where? Where?« cooed the pigeons.

»In the yard across the way. I have as good as seen it myself. It is almost not a proper story to tell, but it's quite true!«

»True, true, every word of it,« said the pigeons, and cooed down into their poultry yard. »There is a hen, and some say there are two hens, who have plucked out all their feathers in order to look different from the rest and to attract the attention of the rooster.«

»Wake up! Wake up!« crowed the rooster, and flew up on the fence. He was still half asleep, but he crowed just the same. »Three hens have died of a broken heart, all for the sake of a rooster, and they have plucked all their feathers out! It's a dreadful story, but I will not keep it to myself. Tell it everywhere!«

»Tell it everywhere!« shrieked the bats; and the hens clucked and the roosters crowed. »Tell it everywhere!«

And so the story travelled from henhouse to henhouse until at last it was carried back to the very same place from where it had really started.

»There are five hens,« now ran the tale, »who all have plucked out all their feathers to show which of them had lost the most weight through unhappy love for their rooster. And then they pecked at each other till they bled and all five dropped dead, to the shame and disgrace of their families, and to the great loss of their owner.«

And the hen who had lost the little loose feather naturally did not recognize her own story; and as she was a respectable hen, she said, »I despise such hens, but there are many of that kind! Such stories should not be hushed up, and I'll do my best to get the story into the newspapers. Then it will be known all over the country; that will serve those hens right, and their families, too.« And it got to the newspapers, and it was printed. And it is quite true. One little feather may grow till it becomes five hens.